READ BETWEEN THE CRIMES

PIPER ASHWELL PSYCHIC P.I., BOOK 2

KELLY HASHWAY

To Ayla with love

CHAPTER ONE

I'm paying for my toasted almond coffee and piece of crumb cake when Detective Mitchell Brennan walks into Marcia's Nook, the bookstore and café next to the office where I work as a private investigator.

"How did I know I'd find you here?" Mitchell asks, walking up to me at the bakery counter.

I use my phone to pay and shake my head at Marcia, my friend and the person who makes sure I remember to eat while I'm at the office. "No case this one can't solve." I jerk a finger in Mitchell's direction. "To think the only evidence he had to go on was the sign on my door that read 'Grabbing breakfast next door. Back in five.'" I pocket my phone and grab my items off the counter.

Marcia smiles at me, used to the way Mitchell and I like to banter. It's been our thing since before we actually decided to be friends. Before my father, former police detective Thomas Ashwell, made Mitchell his partner to ensure there'd be someone on the Weltunkin Police Force who believes in my abilities as a psychometrist and would look after me. That part, I hated, but Mitchell's grown on me—like a fungus that won't go away, so you learn to live with it.

Mitchell sighs and directs his attention to Marcia. "You're looking as beautiful as ever this morning." He leans his forearms on the glass pastry case.

"Always such a charmer, Detective," Marcia says. While she's not oblivious to Mitchell's good looks, she doesn't fawn over him the way most women do. "What can I get for you this morning?"

Mitchell looks at me, cocking his head. "I'll have whatever she's having."

I hold up the bag. "I could have a book in here. Then what would you do? I doubt you've read anything besides a police report since high school."

"It's been since college, but who's counting?" He smirks. "And anyway, Marcia has different bags for the books and the food."

"You're very observant, Detective," Marcia says, bagging up a piece of crumb cake.

"Comes with the job description." Mitchell removes a twenty from his wallet and puts it on the counter.

Marcia caps his to-go cup and rings him up, but he already has his food in hand and is walking toward the exit. "Detective, your change," Marcia calls after him.

Mitchell turns around, pushing the door open with his back. "That's your tip," he says with a smile. "Piper, are you coming?"

Marcia and I exchange shrugs. It's not the first time Mitchell has left her an insanely large tip.

"See you soon," I tell her.

"You know where to find me." She removes her apron and heads to the back, no doubt to get another shipment of books that need to be scanned into the system and shelved.

Mitchell holds the door for me.

"What was with the tip you left for Marcia?" I ask once we're outside. "I thought you weren't interested in dating her."

"I'm not. She's too good for me and my lifestyle."

"*Way* too good."

I expect a reaction from Mitchell, but he doesn't say anything.

In the time it takes to walk the twenty-three steps from Marcia's Nook to my office space in the strip mall on Fifth Street, I wait for Mitchell to tell me why he's here. I know it means there's another case he needs my help with, but I'm not offering my services without him asking. When I worked with my father, he and I used to play this song and dance routine at the start of every new case. It always annoyed me, but now I found myself missing it. Not that Mitchell could ever replace my father, in my life or on the police force. After learning his mother was psychic and foresaw her own death, I've been able to overlook the fact that Mitchell was once a chauvinist pig.

"You're really going to make me do this, aren't you?" Mitchell asks as I unlock my office door and flip the closed sign to "Open."

"Do what?" I step inside and click the light switch. Tossing my purse into the bottom drawer of my desk, I plop down in the chair, setting my breakfast in front of me.

Mitchell takes the seat across from me without prompting. "I'm not sure how to do this exactly. Do I call you 'pumpkin' and tell you I need your help? Is that what your father would have done?"

After removing my crumb cake from the bag, I flatten the bag out and use it as a plate. "That depends if you want your coffee dumped in your lap or not," I say. We've already had the "pumpkin" conversation. My father is the only one who gets away with calling me that.

Mitchell smiles and takes a sip of his coffee. After he swallows, he says, "No, it's definitely too hot for that. I guess I'll just level with you then. We have a case."

We. He's viewing us as partners, which we aren't. Not really. I might be the Weltunkin PD's go-to for missing persons cases, but I'm not anyone's partner. "You mean *you* have a case. Go on."

"You aren't going to make me beg, are you?"

I tilt my head from side to side like I'm considering the idea. "Tell me about the case, and then I'll decide if you need to beg or not." I sip my coffee, needing caffeine to deal with a missing persons case this early in my day. I'd planned to handle small things today, like run the background check on a potential employee for Weltunkin Financial Services.

Mitchell takes a bite of his crumb cake and sits back in his chair, adjusting his hunter green tie. "I'm not even sure how to classify this case."

"I don't see a police report tucked anywhere," I say.

"I didn't bring you one. They don't help you anyway, right?"

Not in the least bit. I need something that belonged to the person. An object I can read. Mitchell's no stranger to my abilities. "What do you have for me then?"

"A story and an address."

I sit back in my chair. "I like stories. Let's see how well you can tell one."

He takes a deep breath before launching into the case. "Steven and Loralei McNamara were married two days ago at the Weltunkin Spa and Resort. They were scheduled to go on their honeymoon to Aruba yesterday, but Loralei never showed up at the airport." He pauses as if that's the end of the story and he's waiting for my reaction.

I wave my hand in the universal gesture for "go on."

He turns up both palms. "That's it. She's missing. The husband has no idea where she is."

I twist the plain silver band on my left pinky. "I'm assuming he's called her relatives and friends to make sure she didn't just decide the marriage was a bad idea and skipped out on the honeymoon."

Mitchell nods. "Steven said no one has heard from her."

"Why didn't the couple go to the airport together?"

"According to Steven, Loralei went back to her apartment to pack, ran late, and called to say she'd meet him at the airport." He narrows his eyes at me. "Are you getting any gut feelings about this?"

"Considering I've never met Loralei or Steven, no. There are plenty of possibilities, though." I down the rest of my coffee and toss the empty cup in the trash can. "You know what I'm going to say."

"I do, and that's why I've already set up a meeting with Steven McNamara. We have twenty minutes to get to his apartment on Westmont Drive." He takes a huge bite of crumb cake, getting crumbs all over the top of my desk.

I shake my head at him. "You're like a child. Could you at least eat over your bag?"

"What?" he asks with his mouth full. "It's crumb cake. Crumbs are to be expected."

"And so is food flying out of your mouth when you talk while you're chewing." I cover the rest of my crumb cake with my hand to keep it from being assaulted by the food spewing out of Mitchell's mouth.

"Sorry." He covers his mouth. Once he swallows and

washes it down with some coffee, he says, "Hurry up and eat so we can get going."

"I've lost my appetite. I'll save this for later." I bag my crumb cake and stand up, grabbing my purse from the drawer. "Let's go."

He crumples the bag and tosses it in the garbage as he stands. Since he can't chug hot coffee the way I can, he brings what's left of it with us. On the way out of the office, Mitchell asks, "Any part of you thinking this Steven guy offed his new bride and is trying to cover it up by reporting her as missing?"

I lock my office door and start for Mitchell's Explorer. "Only one way to find out." I raise a brow at him, and I don't need to tell him my plan. He knows the second I meet Steven McNamara, I'll read him under the pretense of shaking his hand.

CHAPTER TWO

Westmont Drive is about twenty minutes from my office, but with the way Mitchell drives, we arrive in fifteen. I get the impression he's expecting me to read Steven McNamara and close this case in a matter of two minutes tops. That certainly would make things easier, but the closer we get to meeting Steven, the less I believe that will be what happens.

We take the elevator to the third floor to apartment 302. Mitchell knocks on the door, and I stare at the empty space between the peephole and the apartment number. Staring at blank space helps me clear my mind before I try to read anyone or anything.

Steven McNamara is a thin man with wire glasses, and since he's about Mitchell's height, I'd guess he's close to six foot tall. He looks back and forth between Mitchell and me. "Detective Brennan?" he asks.

I give Mitchell the side-eye for not telling Mr. McNamara I was coming along. Although, I know why he didn't. If Mr. McNamara disapproved of my assistance with the case, I wouldn't be able to read him.

"Yes," Mitchell says, extending his hand. It's a smart

move because it sets me up to shake Mr. McNamara's hand as well.

"Mr. McNamara, I'm Piper Ashwell. I'm a private investigator working with the Weltunkin PD to find your wife." I extend my right hand to him.

"Nice to meet you Ms.—" The rest of his words are swallowed by my vision.

"Mom, I waited for two hours. I called her no less than seven times before our flight boarded." Steven twists the wedding band around his finger. "I don't know where she could be. Something must have happened to her. She wouldn't just..." Sobs swallow his words, and he sinks onto the couch. He wipes his nose with the back of his hand.

"Try not to panic, sweetheart. The police will find her. It will be all right."

"We should be on the beach right now, starting our lives together." Steven covers his eyes, his tears dotting his black dress pants.

"Ms. Ashwell?" Steven's voice breaks me out of the vision, and he pulls his hand free.

"I'm sorry," I say, lowering my arm to my side. I look at Mitchell and give the smallest shake of my head, letting him know my vision had nothing to do with Steven doing anything to cause his wife's disappearance.

"She gets a little dizzy sometimes," Mitchell says, trying to cover for me. Though I'm not sure why. I've never hidden my abilities from people.

"Mr. McNamara, could we please come inside for a few moments and ask you a couple questions? I promise we won't take up too much of your time."

He nods and steps aside so we can enter. The apartment is small, a single bedroom judging by the fact that I only see two doors in the living room, which is connected to the small kitchen. One must be the bathroom, leaving the second door to lead to the bedroom. Everything inside the place is brown. It screams bachelor.

I move toward the brown leather couch I saw Steven sitting on in my vision. "Mr. McNamara, I understand you and your wife occupy separate apartments."

"Yes." He runs a hand through his hair. "Loralei didn't want to live together before we were married. She slept here the night of our wedding and then went home in the morning to pack for our flight."

"I see. And what time did she leave in the morning?" I nod to Mitchell, indicating he should take notes and let me lead the questioning. He pulls out his pad and pen and starts scribbling.

Steven lets out a large puff of air. "I think it was around seven. We had a ten o'clock flight." He sits down on the edge of the couch while Mitchell and I stand. I don't want to touch anything while I'm questioning him in fear I'll miss something he says when a vision takes over. There's time enough for that later.

"And what happened after that?"

"I don't know. I was in the shower, and she called me to say she was running late."

"Did she tell you why?" I ask.

"No. I assumed she was struggling with what to pack. She always takes forever to plan her outfits, so I didn't think anything of it."

"How did she seem when you spoke to her?" Mitchell asks.

"She didn't say much and she was a little flustered, but I figured she was trying to pack in a hurry. She knows I like to make sure we're at the airport two hours before the flight.

They tell you to always allow two hours..." His voice trails off.

"What did you do next?" I ask.

"I got dressed, grabbed my suitcase, and went to the airport. I looked everywhere for Loralei, and I called her a few times, but she didn't answer." He lowers his head, staring at his wedding band. "I thought maybe she decided she'd made a mistake in marrying me, so I left her a message telling her..." His shoulders shake, and he doesn't finish the statement.

"Mr. McNamara, would it be okay if I take a look at your phone?" I ask.

"The police already checked my call records," he says, removing the phone from his back pocket and handing it to me.

I take it with my left hand at first, not wanting to read the energy off the phone just yet. It's time to tell Mr. McNamara what I can do. "Mr. McNamara, I'm not your ordinary private investigator. I'm what's referred to as a psychometrist. I can read energy off objects and people and get clues that are useful in cases like your wife's."

He shakes his head and narrows his eyes at me. "I'm sorry, but I don't understand."

"She's psychic," Mitchell says, putting it into terms most people are familiar with. "She's helped the Weltunkin PD solve a lot of missing persons cases by reading objects. She can use your phone to bring on a vision that might help us locate your wife."

Mr. McNamara couldn't look more skeptical, so I say, "It's best if I just show you." I transfer the phone to my right hand.

"Loralei, I don't know where you are or why you won't answer my calls or texts, but if this is about... If you're

thinking you made a mistake, just talk to me. I won't be angry. We don't have to go on our honeymoon, but please talk to me. Let me try to fix this. I love you."

"What's happening?" Mr. McNamara asks, looking at Mitchell. "I don't know what I'm supposed to be seeing here."

I hand the phone back to him. "What were you trying to fix, Mr. McNamara?"

Mitchell's head whips in Steven's direction.

"You told Loralei you wanted her to let you 'try to fix this.' What did you mean by that?"

"How did you...?" Mr. McNamara's gaze lowers to his phone in his hand. "You heard my phone conversation?"

"Yes. I can't begin to explain my abilities to you. Just know they're very real. Now if you could please answer my question."

"I-I just meant we needed to talk through whatever was bothering her."

"And you have no idea what that was?" He's hiding something. I can feel it.

"We weren't engaged for long, so I thought maybe she felt like we'd rushed into marriage. I was willing to go to counseling or whatever she wanted to fix it." He returns his phone to his pocket and stands up, not meeting my gaze. He walks around me, making me feel like he's deliberately putting distance between us.

"Mr. McNamara, now that you're aware I can read people as well as objects, I'm going to guess that you've figured out why I held our handshake for so long."

He whirls around on me. "Don't you need a search warrant to invade someone's privacy like that?"

I repress the urge to scoff. I'd need a search warrant for every person I ever came into contact with if that were the case. I move toward him, and he backs up into the kitchen island. Out of the corner of my eye, I see Mitchell smirk. "I saw how distraught you were over your wife's disappearance. That reading is the only reason why I'm not suggesting we bring you to the police station for further questioning."

"I don't understand," Steven says.

"You're obviously hiding something, and Piper can see that," Mitchell spells it out for him. "I'm not psychic, and I can see you're deliberately keeping something from us."

"Fine. It's not what you think, though. I love my wife."

"I know you do," I say to reassure him. The problem is love makes people do crazy things. Or so I've seen.

Steven leans against the island for support. "I'm not exactly Loralei's type, but her parents wanted her to be with someone like me. I knew that, and I used it to my advantage. You see, I work with Loralei's father. He's the one who introduced us at a work party. Loralei is so far out of my league. She's beautiful. And I'm..." He gestures to his too-thin frame. "I'm successful, though. I only live in this tiny apartment because I've been saving all my money to buy a house off of Millington Way."

I'm familiar with Millington Way. My last case involved the nineteen-year-old daughter of a wealthy businessman named Victor Castell. He lived at the top of Millington Way in the largest house I've ever seen. "Property there costs a pretty penny," I say.

"I know, but it was a wedding present for Loralei. The moving company was scheduled to bring all our belongings to the new house while we were on our honeymoon. That way we could return to Weltunkin and start our lives together in our new home." He stands up fully and moves toward me. "I still want that. I want her back. Please find her. Find her and tell her I'm sorry."

"Sorry for what exactly?" Mitchell asks.

"I proposed to her in front of both our parents because I knew she'd never say no with them present."

He manipulated her. If I hadn't already read him against his will, I'd do it now just out of spite.

"I could see why you'd think she'd figure that out and run," Mitchell says, and it's clear his opinion of Steven just plummeted as well.

"Do you have a key to Loralei's apartment?" I ask, wanting to move on with this investigation and get away from Steven McNamara before I tell him exactly what I think of him.

"Yeah, I have a key."

"Do we have your permission to search her apartment?" Mitchell asks.

Steven's name most likely isn't on the lease, so his permission isn't necessary. The fact that he's asking is just his way of making sure Steven really does want us looking for information about Loralei's whereabouts. Knowing Mitchell, he probably assumes Steven and Loralei fought about his proposal technique and he did something to her.

"It's her apartment. What I think doesn't really matter, does it?" Steven asks, opening the top drawer in the kitchen and removing a key.

"No," I say, holding out my hand, palm up.

He's careful not to touch me when he places the key in my open palm. Coward.

"Thank you for your help, Mr. McNamara. We'll be in touch." I start for the door.

"You have my number if you should remember anything that might be helpful in solving this case," Mitchell says.

I reach for the doorknob, but before I can turn it, another vision hits me.

Loralei's left hand is on the doorknob, and she stares at the wedding band on her finger. Heartache fills her, bringing tears to her eyes. "What have I done?" she whispers, looking back at the bedroom door before hurrying out of the apartment.

Mitchell's hand is on the small of my back. "Everything okay?" he says in a soft voice so Steven doesn't overhear.

I open the door and step into the hallway. Mitchell closes the door behind us, and I start for the elevator.

"What did you see?"

"Loralei. The morning she left that apartment." I make sure Steven isn't coming out of his apartment before saying, "She didn't want to marry him, and she was filled with regret."

"So you think she ran?" Mitchell asks.

"I think there's a damn good chance she did."

CHAPTER THREE

Instead of driving us to Loralei's apartment, Mitchell pulls into his own condo. I almost don't realize at first because my head is back against the headrest and my eyes are closed for the entire ride.

"What are you doing?" I ask as he cuts the engine.

He gives me an admonishing glare. "You really expected to go to Loralei's apartment and have another vision after you just had three with Steven McNamara?"

I shrug. "It's kind of my job. If you didn't need my visions, I wouldn't be in this vehicle with you right now."

"I know that, but I also know your visions take a toll on you. You need some downtime to recover." He gets out of the Explorer and closes the door as if this conversation is over.

I push my door open and follow him into the condo. "You know, just because you've witnessed me having a few visions doesn't make you an expert on them or my keeper. Even my father didn't try to coddle me this much."

"Who are you trying to fool? I had a front row seat to your father babying you after a vision. I know exactly what he would say to you right now." He tosses his keys on the kitchen counter and opens the refrigerator. He grabs two bottles of water and tosses one to me.

"You think working one case alongside my father and me told you everything about our relationship?"

"No, *I* did." Dad walks out of Mitchell's bathroom, completely blindsiding me.

"What are you doing here?" I ask as he comes over and hugs me.

"Mitchell texted me."

"And how did you happen to be inside his locked condo?"

"Despite working in law enforcement, Mitchell has a hidden key outside." Dad takes the key from his jeans pocket and tosses it to Mitchell. "Don't let me find that next time I'm here. Now that my daughter seems to frequent this place, it's not safe to have a key anyone can find."

"I don't frequent Mitchell's condo, Dad. We're working a case, and I had no idea he was bringing me here. More to the point though, you can't just show up at Mitchell's place, let yourself in, and start bossing him around. He's a grown man."

"It's fine, Piper," Mitchell says. "I invited him and told him where the key was so he could let himself in instead of waiting in his car."

I throw my arms out, not sure how I'm stuck in the middle of these two yet again. "How's retirement treating you?" I ask Dad.

"Nobody mentioned the part where it was boring as all hell. Your mother practically kicked me out the door when I told her about Mitchell's text."

I cross my arms. "And what was the content of the text?"

READ BETWEEN THE CRIMES

Dad approaches me and grips both of my arms. "Piper, you know I love you, but you are stubborn. You get that from your mother, but don't you dare tell her I said that."

"Funny because Mom said the exact same thing to me last week except she said I get it from you."

"Fine." Dad rolls his eyes. "We're both stubborn. There was no hope for you, which is why you need to listen to Mitchell."

I burst out laughing. "Listen to Mitchell about my visions. That's rich, Dad."

"I'm not joking, Piper. Three visions in quick succession can do you in. We both know that's true."

"Except these visions were mild. They were about broken hearts, not murders."

Dad cocks his head. "And when was the last time you had a broken heart?"

It's a low blow considering we both know I don't date. I can't date. I avoid getting close to anyone because of my abilities. One goodnight kiss could reveal more to me than my date would ever want me to know about him.

"I figured you might need some help with this one."

"This vision or this case?" I ask. "Are you taking me up on my offer to come work with me?"

Dad puts one hand in the air. "I'm not saying I'll come on board for every case, but your mother has a desk picked out for me already. She said it will fit perfectly in your office next to yours. The chair even has extra lumbar support."

I nudge Dad's arm with my elbow. "I knew you'd cave."

"I'm not doing any paperwork or trudging through forests in the middle of the night. Those days are long over." He wags a finger in my face.

"Whatever you say, Dad."

Mitchell motions for us to take a seat on the couch, and

he sits in the chair. "So, fill us in on these visions. How much do you know?"

"Not much. Steven McNamara loves his wife, but he completely manipulated her and she's aware of it. She doesn't love him. Yet..." I press my hand to my chest. "I don't know. What I felt when I saw her, it was like her insides were tearing apart."

Dad nods and pats my knee. "Pumpkin, it's called a broken heart for a reason."

God, I'm glad I never experienced this firsthand. At least I know what I'm feeling now isn't real. It's just a reflection of what Loralei felt. "What I don't understand is why she felt like this if she never loved Steven."

"How do you know she didn't love him at one point?" Mitchell asks, leaning forward and resting his forearms on his thighs. "Maybe she did and that's why she agreed to marry him, but she fell out of love with him and realized it too late, when she had already said 'I do.'"

"Can you really fall out of love with someone that quickly?" I ask, my gaze going to Dad because I'm not sure Mitchell knows any more about being in love than I do.

Dad rubs his jaw. "Well, there is the expression 'there's a thin line between love and hate.' That had to come from somewhere."

Is it possible what I'm feeling is hatred? No, that's an emotion I'm familiar with. "It isn't hate," I say, twirling the ring on my finger. "But she definitely did regret marrying Steven. She was looking at her ring and asking herself 'What did I do?'"

"Do you think she married him for the money and the life he could provide her? Maybe she realized she wanted love more in the end?" Mitchell's words come out like he's thinking aloud instead of asking for our opinions on the matter.

"That could be," Dad says. "But why not ask for a divorce or an annulment?"

My chest tightens as I think about the vision. "There's love there. I can feel it."

"And the pained expression on your face says you don't like feeling it," Mitchell says.

"It's awful." I press one hand to my chest and the other to my head. "Maybe I'm seeing overlapping visions again." It wouldn't be the first time, and it's confusing when it happens because I have no idea which pieces go with which vision.

"I think you need to focus on one specific thing at a time," Dad says. "You're trying to read too much at once."

"Like I told Mitchell, I need to go to Loralei's apartment. Maybe I could read her wedding dress." That should tell me how she really felt on the day of her wedding. Her emotions will be tied to the dress.

"Fine, then that will be our next step. But first drink your water, and I'll order us some food. What's everyone in the mood for?" Mitchell asks.

My eyes go to the clock on the cable box under the TV. It's past noon already. I rub my forehead. Losing track of time from my visions isn't anything new to me. In fact, I lose track of time most days.

Dad and Mitchell are discussing food options, so I drink my water and focus on clearing my mind. I keep seeing Loralei's wedding ring in my head. For some reason, I can't shake the image of it.

———

An hour later, I'm standing inside Loralei's apartment on Zinnia Court. Unlike Steven's apartment, Loralei's is full of vibrant colors. The walls are rich yellows, blues, and reds, and every table and counter has a vase of fresh flowers. Immediately, I get the sense that Loralei is full of life. She sees the beauty in the world and embraces it.

"She's nothing like Steven," I say aloud.

Mitchell touches a lace doily under the vase of flowers on the kitchen table. "They definitely have very different senses of style."

"Yes, but you know what they say about opposites attracting," Dad chimes in, opening the stainless steel refrigerator door. "Not much food in here, but I suppose that's to be expected since she planned to go away for a week on her honeymoon."

I walk toward the bedroom, my destination being the closet in hopes her wedding dress is inside. The room is definitely the prettiest in the apartment. The bed is situated in the center of the back wall. The bedspread is floral with so many pillows I'm not sure how Loralei ever slept in the bed. There are several paintings on the walls, all of flowers. "Guess you have a thing for flowers, huh, Loralei?" I say, running my left hand over one of the canvases.

I move toward the white closet doors, which are huge considering the closet runs the entire length of the right wall. Designer clothing and handbags fill the space. Loralei sure didn't marry Steven for his money if she was able to buy all of this herself. I can't imagine him having bought all this in the short time they were engaged. I flip through the clothing, looking for a garment bag that might contain her wedding dress, but I reach the end and come up empty.

I decide to check the nightstand. Maybe she kept a journal and wrote all her true feelings in it. Does anyone keep journals anymore? The top drawer contains a small dish for jewelry, a sleep mask, contraceptives, and breath mints. I close it and open the second drawer. This one has lingerie and other undergarments.

Mitchell walks into the room and leans on the door-frame. "Anything?"

I shake my head. "I was hoping to find her wedding dress. That should be able to tell me exactly how she felt about marrying Steven."

Mitchell stands up straight and tips his head in the direction of the kitchen. "Your father found a dry cleaning ticket in the kitchen drawer. She's having the dress cleaned."

Damn. I might not be able to get a read off it after it's cleaned. "When did she drop it off?" Maybe I could inter-cept the dress before it's cleaned.

"The morning after the wedding. Why? Are you plan-ning to pose as Loralei and pick it up, because I'm pretty sure they'd remember what she looks like?"

"I could say I'm picking it up for her since she's away. Having the ticket should be proof enough."

Mitchell shrugs. "Worth a shot, I suppose."

We meet my father in the living room. He's sitting on the couch flipping through some sort of notebook. "Any luck in here?" I ask him.

"She kept a day planner. Everything in here looks typi-cal. Hair and nail appointments, rehearsal dinner"—he flips the page—"and the flight time for the honeymoon."

"Can I see that?" I sit down next to him and reach for the planner. I focus on the day of the wedding and place my right palm flat against the words "Wedding day."

Loralei taps her pen against the page, the cap hitting the word "wedding" over and over again. Her stomach flips.

*"Just prewedding jitters. Totally normal," she assures herself.
"Tomorrow I'll be Mrs. Steven McNamara."*

*A memory tugs at her mind. She was thirteen years old
and doodling in a notebook in school while her history
teacher lectured. She wrote "Loralei Graham" and "Mrs.
Loralei Graham" in the margins with little hearts dotting the
I in her name.*

Her chest constricts, and she starts crying.

"Piper?" Dad's arm is around me, and he's gently
rocking me back and forth. "What did you see?"

I blink a few times, and tears spill down my cheeks. I
wipe them away, and Mitchell hands me a tissue before
sitting down next to me.

"I'm guessing you were right and she didn't want to
marry him," Mitchell says.

"I'm not sure. The vision started out being about him,
but then it changed. She was young. Thirteen. For some
reason I know she was thirteen. And she was writing 'Mrs.
Loralei Graham' in her notebook. She was just a kid
dreaming about marrying the boy she had a crush on. It
could mean anything," I say.

"Or it could mean she wished she was marrying this
Graham guy instead," Mitchell suggests, getting to his feet.
"Maybe we should search for old yearbooks and find out
who this guy is."

"That means putting the dry cleaner on hold," I say.
"I'm not sure if that's a good idea."

"Let's hit the dry cleaner first," Dad says, standing and
offering me a hand. "If that turns out to be a dead end, we
can come back here and search for the yearbooks."

Dad grabs the dry cleaner ticket from the kitchen
drawer, and we head out. Dad drives, so I ride shotgun,
while Mitchell takes the back seat. I'm used to Mitchell

forcing me to take the back seat, but I guess he's feeling sympathetic after all the visions I've been having. My head is throbbing with the beginning of a headache, but I don't dare take aspirin when I know I need to be able to read that dress still today. I can't have anything clouding my brain's natural ability to sense energy.

Alberto's Dry Cleaners is on Main Street, sandwiched between a tuxedo rental place and an antique shop called Golden Oldies. As soon as Dad puts the car in park, I hop out and rush inside the dry cleaner.

No one is at the counter, so I ring the bell.

"Just a second," comes a thick Italian accent.

I look around at the rack of clothing behind the counter. No wedding dresses. I'm not sure if that's a good or bad thing.

A man in his late forties with a graying beard emerges and smiles at me. "I am Alberto. What can I do for you today?" He looks at my empty hands, and then his gaze goes to Mitchell and Dad standing behind me.

I produce the ticket from my pocket. "I need to pick up the wedding dress my friend Loralei McNamara dropped off. She's on her honeymoon and asked me to get it for her."

Alberto examines the ticket. "What timing. I just finished cleaning it." He holds up a finger and disappears into the back room again.

My shoulders slump.

"Sorry, pumpkin," Dad says. "But don't get too discouraged. You might still be able to get a read off it."

Alberto returns with the dress in a white garment bag. "Here you are. Good as new. And Mrs. McNamara paid ahead of time, so you don't owe anything."

"Thanks," I say, reaching for the garment bag. I bring it out to Dad's car and get into the passenger seat. While Dad and Mitchell get in the car, I focus on clearing my mind. Then I unzip the bag and reach for the dress. Holding it in my right hand, I close my eyes and wait for the vision.

But I can't see anything. The sharp, sweet smell of perchloroethylene Alberto used to clean the garment is the only whisper of a memory I get from the dress.

Another dead end.

CHAPTER FOUR

Back at Loralei's apartment, we all search for old yearbooks. This mystery Graham guy is our only lead now that the dress yielded no memories of Loralei or her wedding day. It's not to say there aren't any memories attached to the dress anymore, but my overactive sense of smell is overriding my ability to read anything but the dry cleaning chemical off it.

"There are some boxes in the top of her closet," I tell Dad and Mitchell. "Can one of you get them down for me?"

"I will," Mitchell says, following me into the bedroom. He motions to the bed. "Hey, did you try reading the bed?"

I eye the floral bedspread and shake my head. "I try to avoid reading anything that could be sexual in nature. It's not a pleasant experience for me."

Mitchell knows I've read a bed before, but that was because I couldn't find anything else to get a good read off of. It's a last resort.

He grabs two boxes from the top of the closet and places them on the bed. I start rifling through one while he goes through the other.

"I found a high school yearbook," he says, holding it up.

Most of the kids Loralei was in middle school with should have gone to high school with her, barring anyone who moved or switched to homeschooling. I take the yearbook and search the index for Loralei when I realize I don't know her maiden name.

"What's Loralei's maiden name?" I ask Mitchell.

"Allen."

I find her in the index and flip to her photograph. It's a senior portrait. "Here's to hoping this Graham guy was in the same grade as her." In high school, a lot of girls in my class fawned over the upperclassman. If that was the case with Loralei, we might not be able to track down her crush. I flip to the last names beginning with G. Gaffney, Gardner, Garrett, Gibbons, Gilbert, Gillen, Gleeson, Glenn, Goode, Gorman, Graham.

I point to his picture. "Elijah Graham." His dark eyes seem to stare up at me from the page.

"Can you get a read off the picture?" Mitchell asks.

How much I can see depends on Loralei's connection to him. If he touched the yearbook to sign it, that would help, too. I study the picture, keeping my hand on it without covering Elijah's face.

Basketball.

Football.

Homecoming king.

Student body president.

I sigh in frustration. "Nothing helpful. The guy was popular and well liked. Nominated and won every title imaginable. That's all I'm getting. It could mean Loralei didn't have a connection to him in high school, other than her crush."

"We should still check him out," Dad says. He's on his

phone in the doorway. "There's an Elijah Graham living in East Stroudsburg. According to his Facebook profile, he attended Weltunkin High School. It has to be our guy."

"I'm assuming you have an address," Mitchell says.

The look Dad gives him makes me laugh.

"Let's go," Dad says.

I nudge Mitchell with my elbow. "You got the 'dad' look. You're in trouble."

"When did he become my father, too?" he asks with a roll of his eyes.

"Wait until he sends you to your room with no dinner," I say.

"Are you two coming, or do I have to do everything on my own?" Dad calls from the front door.

"We're coming," I say, and Mitchell and I exchange a look.

East Stroudsburg isn't far from Weltunkin, so it only takes about thirty minutes to drive there. Elijah Graham lives on the upper end of East Stroudsburg, away from the college and near an abandoned resort. Dad pulls into a community that isn't gated but has a security guard sitting in a car at the entrance.

Mitchell flashes his badge at the guy, who couldn't appear to care less about our presence. His feet are propped up on the dashboard, and his seat is almost fully reclined. "Well, there's a waste of the homeowners' dues."

I nod in agreement as Dad turns right and drives up a small hill. He follows the road to the end and pulls down a driveway in front of a white Victorian with black shutters. He cuts the engine. "Ready or not, we're here."

We all get out and walk up the front porch to the door. Mitchell rings the doorbell, and a dog immediately starts barking. Most animals can sense my abilities. The only one

I've ever encountered who didn't like that was my parents' dog, Max. Maybe it's because he's notorious for chewing shoes and I always know when he's about to hijack one of Mom's slippers.

I recognize Elijah Graham the second he opens the door. The years have been kind to him. He takes in our appearance and runs a hand through his hair. "Can I help you?"

A golden retriever bounds toward us, barking.

"Jezebel, sit!" Elijah says, and the dog's backside drops to the floor.

"Impressive," I say, bending down to the dog's level. "Hi, Jezebel. You're a very pretty girl."

Elijah furrows his brow at me. "I'm sorry, but I was in the middle of something, so could we maybe hurry this along? If you're selling something, I'm not interested."

Mitchell flashes his badge, and Elijah shuts up.

"I'm Detective Brennan. This is Detective Ashwell and his daughter, Piper Ashwell."

"I'm a private investigator," I add, rubbing Jezebel's head. She drops to the ground and rolls over so she's belly up. "Who likes her belly rubbed?" I say in a baby voice.

"Am I in some sort of trouble?" Elijah asks.

"What would make you think that?" Dad cocks his head and gives Elijah an intimidating stare.

"Well, I have an unpaid parking ticket, but I can't think of anything else that would bring you here."

"This isn't about a parking ticket, Mr. Graham," I say, standing up. "We're here because a former classmate of yours is missing."

"I haven't kept in touch with any of my former class-mates." Elijah pauses, and his eyes gaze off well above our heads, like he's trying to remember something. "No. I can't think of anyone."

"Not even Loralei Allen?" I ask.

"Loralei? I don't even remember anyone by that name."

"Are you certain?" Dad asks. "It's an uncommon name. I'd think you'd remember it since you and Loralei were in the same class."

"Have you seen the size of Weltunkin High School? The place is gigantic. I didn't know half the people in my graduating class. I remember being at graduation and wondering who the hell some of those people were."

"You were very involved in the school, Mr. Graham. How is it possible that the student body president, homecoming king,"—I tick them off on my fingers—"star football player, and star basketball player didn't know his classmates?"

Elijah sighs. "I was popular, yes, but that's my point. People knew me. That doesn't mean I knew them."

Why would Loralei have a crush on someone as self-centered as Elijah? Something isn't adding up. "Mr. Graham, thank you for your time," I say, earning me questioning looks from both Mitchell and my father. I extend my right hand to Elijah.

His face scrunches in confusion, but he shakes my hand.

"You can't tell anyone about this. I mean it. Not a word to any of your friends. It never happened." Elijah looks out the window at the dark parking lot.

Loralei nods. "Not a word."

Elijah hesitates for a moment and then kisses her.

I let go of Elijah's hand. "Why did you want your relationship with her to be a secret?" I ask.

He steps back, and his gaze falls on my hand, which is still outstretched. "How...?"

"I neglected to tell you that I'm a psychic PI. *Psychic* being the key word there." I cross my arms. "You were seeing Loralei Allen in secret. Why?"

Elijah lets out a huff. "Fine. I hung out with her a few times in private. She was a nobody at that school. I couldn't be seen with her or it might have cost me my reputation. I wasn't willing to risk that, and she was fine with it."

He isn't lying about that. Loralei didn't seem to mind them dating in secret. In fact, I got the sense she found it thrilling.

"I haven't seen her since high school. I swear." He pauses and then reaches his hand out to me. "Do you need to be touching me to tell if I'm lying? If so, go right ahead. I'm not hiding anything."

"Why were you afraid to tell us about your relationship with Loralei?" Mitchell asks.

Elijah shrugs. "Old habits, I suppose. And I had no idea you had a psychic working with you."

"Is there anything else you'd like to tell us, Mr. Graham," Dad asks. "You're certain you haven't had any contact of any kind with Loralei? No phone calls, texts, emails...?"

Elijah shakes his head. "None. She was a high school hookup. Nothing more. I'm not even sure why you're here questioning me about her."

"We have to look into every possible lead," Mitchell says. "Loralei still lives in Weltunkin. You're here, which is plenty close enough to keep in touch. You can see how we'd connect the dots."

"Sure. Are we finished here now?" He jerks a thumb over his shoulder. "I have an appointment to get ready for."

Mitchell pulls a card from his pocket. "If you should hear from Loralei, give me a call."

Elijah scans the card and nods. "I will, but like I said, I haven't talked to her since high school. I don't think I'll be any help to your case."

"We appreciate your time," I say, bending down to pat Jezebel on the head again before walking back to Dad's BMW.

Once we're on the road heading back to Weltunkin, Mitchell asks, "So what do you make of that? Was he telling the truth?"

"Yeah. He and Loralei were in a dark parking lot in my vision."

"What a jerk," Mitchell says. "He'd lower himself to sleeping with someone he deemed not good enough for his social status, but he wouldn't let her tell anyone about it."

"I think she liked the arrangement. I could tell she was..." I searched for the right word.

"Turned on by it?" Mitchell offers.

Dad glares at him in the rearview mirror, and Mitchell shrugs. "I'm only trying to help."

"She liked sneaking around and the prospect of being caught," I say. "Maybe that was the problem with her relationship with Steven. Even her parents approved of him. He was safe." Too safe for Loralei's liking.

"That makes sense. But if that's why she ran, where did she go? We can't solve this case until we figure that out." Mitchell sits forward in the seat and stares at me as if the answer will magically come to me.

I widen my eyes at him. "What are you expecting me to read here?"

"I was hoping you'd just get a gut feeling," he says.

"Piper, remember the game we used to play when you were younger?" Dad asks.

I take a deep breath, knowing exactly what he's referring to. It's designed to get me to clear my mind of all thoughts. He starts asking me random questions I know the answers to. Once I fall into a rhythm, he throws in questions pertaining to the case, and if I'm lucky, the answer comes to me.

I lean my head back and close my eyes.

"Is this a sleeping game?" Mitchell asks.

I open the eye closest to him and say, "Shush."

He mouths, "Sorry," and I close my eye again.

Dad waits while I take deep, soothing yoga breaths. Inhale and count to eight. Exhale and count to ten. Okay, they're yoga breaths taken to the extreme, but I need to be really relaxed in a hurry. Soon I do feel like I could fall asleep, and Dad must sense it because he begins with the questions.

"Have you done laundry in the past week?"

"No."

"Is Rose your middle name?"

"Yes."

"Is your favorite color purple?"

"Yes."

"Are you a private investigator?"

"Yes."

"Did Loralei McNamara run away?"

"No."

"Did something happen to her on the morning she was supposed to go on her honeymoon?"

"Yes."

"Do you know what that was?"

"She was kidnapped."

CHAPTER FIVE

When I open my eyes, Mitchell is still sitting forward as far as his seat belt will allow and staring at me.

"She was kidnapped? Do you know by whom?"

"Did you miss the part where my eyes are now open and I'm no longer in my peaceful meditative state?" I rub my forehead. Sometimes I can't control when I come out of that state. It happens because my mind is jolted by the shock of what just presented itself to me.

"Can we try it again?" he asks.

"Mitchell, that's enough. Piper can't see everything. She works best when she has objects to read."

That's always been where my strength lies. I wish I was one of those psychics who could just talk to their spirit guides and get answers. I don't really work that way. I just know certain things to be true, or I read objects, people, or animals.

"Do you think she was kidnapped from her apartment?" Mitchell asks.

"No," I say without hesitation. "I would have sensed

that when we were there. Nothing bad happened at her apartment."

"Then maybe she saw someone before she left or she went somewhere. The dry cleaners?" Mitchell suggests.

My head hurts and I don't want to snap at him, but it's been a long day and I'd think he'd catch on by now. "I was just there. Again, I would have sensed something."

"Time to get you home to bed, pumpkin," Dad says. "You need your rest."

He could say that again. This day has felt more like a week.

"We'll reconvene tomorrow morning at eight in your office," Dad says. "Or should I say *our* office?"

"When is your desk arriving?" I ask.

"Between the hours of ten and two. I might have to stay behind to sign for it."

I wave my hand in the air. "I could ask Marcia to sign for it and let them in if we need to go out. She's done it for me before." Thank God for Marcia. She's definitely someone I can rely on.

"Great. Then rest up because we need that noggin of yours in tiptop shape in the morning." Dad pulls into my apartment complex and drives right up to the front door. "How's Theo doing? Have you seen him lately?"

Theodore Hall owns my apartment complex and is one of Dad's oldest friends. That's the reason why I can afford to live in a wealthy town like Weltunkin. "He's fine. I'll tell him you said hello." I get out of the car, and to my surprise, so does Mitchell.

"I'll walk you to the door."

"The whole fifteen feet?" I ask.

Mitchell gently takes me by the elbow and whispers, "Are you sure you're okay?"

I grab the door handle but don't pull it open. "It's just been a long day. I'll be fine after a good eight hours of sleep. Now go before my father gets the wrong idea about us."

Mitchell laughs. "Yeah, he's been on my case more than usual."

"Then stop doing things like walking me to the door, and go back to being your usual annoying self." I give a small wave and head into the building.

Dad doesn't know the full story about Mitchell's mother foreseeing her own death and choosing to die anyway. I had the misfortune of seeing that memory of his from his mother's perspective. It was difficult, but not nearly as awful as it was for Mitchell to deal with. His need to constantly ask me how I am stems from his desire to go back in time and save his mother. Or at the very least to stop me from ending up like her. While I understand it, it isn't easy for me to deal with.

Upstairs in my apartment, I crawl into bed without even bothering to shower or change. I just want sleep to take me so I can forget about this case and let the peace of ignorance wash over me for a few hours.

———

The bell over the door at Marcia's Nook jingles, announcing my entrance. "Shh. Too early," I say as if the bell will be quieter at my plea.

"Good morning," Marcia says, putting a new tray of jelly donuts in the bakery case.

"It's morning, but it's not good."

"Up late reading again?" She shakes her finger at me. "Don't make me cut you off, Piper. You need your rest."

"I wish that was it. Speaking of, I need a new book."

Reading helps me unwind. It's also my go-to activity on nights I'm not working cases since I'm lacking in the friend department.

"I just shelved some new mysteries. Check the display on the end of the aisle. I'll get your coffee while you look."

I hold up three fingers. "I need three. One toasted almond for me and two dark roast for my father and Detective Brennan." I walk down the rows of books to the mystery section.

"I thought your trio had become a duo," Marcia calls to me.

"Tell that to the man who doesn't know the definition of 'retirement.'" I scan the new titles, honing in on one with a blue cover.

Something borrowed, something blue.

I shake my head, not sure where that thought came from. I grab the book and bring it to the counter.

"I bagged up some pastries for you guys as well," Marcia says. "On the house."

"That's not necessary. Let me pay for them." I take out my phone, ready to pay my bill.

"You can pay for the book, but after all the tips Detective Brennan has left me lately, you are not paying for the coffee and pastries."

I hand her the book. "Fine."

She scans it, and I use my phone to pay.

"Oh, I almost forgot. My father is having a desk delivered today. He's going to be working with me now instead of the Weltunkin PD."

"That's great. You two always made such a great team."

"Yeah. But we might be out when the delivery guys show up."

"Say no more," Marcia says. "Put a sign on your door

telling them to come here. I'll let them in and sign for the delivery."

"You're the best," I say, getting my spare office key from my purse and dropping it into her outstretched hand. "And thank you for breakfast as well." I put a five-dollar bill in the tip jar before grabbing the bag and cup carrier. I don't usually carry cash, but since Marcia is always giving me free food, I've made it a point to have some money for tips.

"I swear I make more in tips from you and Detective Brennan than I do from all my other customers combined," she calls after me.

"Only because we love you," I say, using my back to open the door and let myself out.

She shakes her head at me, but any form of reprimand is lost in the smile that creeps across her face.

Dad and Mitchell are both standing in front of my office when I arrive.

"I'll take that," Mitchell says, reaching for the bag. "What goodies did Marcia give us today?" He immediately peeks inside. "Chocolate chip cannolis. I really love that woman."

"Once again, she's way too good for you," I say, unlocking the door.

"I'm going to need a key, Piper," Dad says.

"Right now, Marcia has it. She's going to let the delivery guys in with your desk." I flip the light switch and walk over to my desk. After placing the cup carrier on the desk and putting my purse in the bottom drawer, I sit down and reach for my toasted almond coffee. "Any new developments while I slept last night?" I ask.

"None," Mitchell says. "Steven McNamara called me for an update. I didn't fill him in on your revelation. I figured it was too soon for that, but I did ask for a list of anyone who Loralei might have said goodbye to before leaving on their honeymoon. He's going to email it to me sometime this morning."

"All right, how about we go over what we know." I lean back in my chair. "Loralei married Steven even though she didn't love him. She regretted her decision, which could lead to her running away, but I know she was kidnapped. So how did she go from trying to run to being kidnapped?" My eyes volley between Mitchell and Dad.

Dad leans his elbows on my desk and steeples his fingers in front of his face. "We'll need a list of wedding guests. It could have been someone who was in town for the wedding."

"But wouldn't Loralei have gone willingly with them to get away from Steven?" Mitchell asks.

"Maybe, unless this was a friend or relative she didn't particularly care for but felt obligated to invite to the wedding," Dad says.

"If you can get a list of names from Steven, one will jump out at me if it's our kidnapper," I say.

"I'm on it." Mitchell stands up and grabs his phone from his pocket. In seconds, he's talking to Steven.

Dad reaches for my left hand. "You okay, pumpkin?"

I rub my forehead with my free hand. "Yeah, it's just that this case is stumping me. Loralei married Steven because it was what her parents wanted her to do. But I keep feeling this heartache. If Elijah wasn't the man who broke Loralei's heart, why did I see his name in my vision?"

Dad doesn't ask if I think Elijah is the kidnapper. He knows I would have sensed that upon meeting Elijah. "Could it be as simple as Loralei believing at one time that she'd marry Elijah?"

This vision feels more metaphorical than that. "I think

Elijah represents something. He's not at all like Steven. He was dangerous in Loralei's mind because they had to sneak around."

"And her relationship with Steven was the exact opposite," Dad says. "It was safe, and everyone knew and approved of it."

"Which she hated." It comes to me as a truth. "She didn't like safe. She wanted...adventure."

Mitchell walks back over to us, pocketing his phone. "Steven said the wedding planner at the Weltunkin Spa and Resort has the list. She took care of everything from invites to seating arrangements to thank you notes. He's calling her now to give us approval to view that information and any other information pertaining to the wedding."

This is good. Going to the site of the wedding is a great idea. "I'll need access to the ballroom where the wedding reception took place and also where they were married, if that was somewhere else."

Dad squeezes my hand. "Piper, are you up for this? I mean, this could be sensory overload for you."

I have to be. I'm not leaving that resort without the vision I need. Still, he's right about this many visions having a serious effect on me. I might need massive amounts of sleep to recover. "I don't really have a choice, Dad." Mitchell won't get much, if anything, from going to the resort. Even a list of names wouldn't be much help because he can't possibly interview everyone who attended the wedding. At least not in a timely manner. Who knows where the kidnapper could take Loralei by then? We don't even know why she was kidnapped. Was it for money? Does the kidnapper intend to kill her?

"Shall we?" Mitchell asks, grabbing his coffee and shoving his cannoli into his mouth.

Dad and I polish off our breakfast while Mitchell drives to the resort, which is situated on a pristine lake. The golf course on the property is frequented by celebrities and has hosted several PGA tournaments. The massive driveway leading to the five-star resort is lined with spiral pine trees and lights. It looks like something you'd see on a tropical island, but given that Weltunkin is a vacation hot spot for celebrities, everything here is upscale.

"I've never been here before," Mitchell says. "It's very impressive." He's staring out the window at the golf course. "I don't even golf, but I want to looking at this course."

I focus on my breathing, trying to center myself and prepare for the barrage of visions I'm going to need to have. Mitchell pulls up to the gated entrance before the resort itself.

"Can I help you?" the security guard manning the booth asks.

Mitchell flashes his badge. "I'm Detective Brennan. These are my associates, Detective Ashwell and Piper Ashwell. We are here with permission from Steven McNamara to investigate his wife's missing persons case."

"Who exactly are you here to see?" the guard asks.

"A wedding planner by the name of Miriam King," Mitchell says.

"One moment." The guard picks up his phone, presumably to call Miriam and check our story. A few moments later, the gate rises and the guard says, "Take your first right to the wedding registry building. It's the small building with the red roof."

"Thank you," Mitchell says.

The resort is made up of several buildings. I'm assuming the largest is the hotel portion while the smaller buildings are rented out for weddings and other functions. I spot a building with a red roof. "Right over there."

"I see it." Mitchell pulls up to the building and finds an open parking spot near the door.

No sooner do I step out of the car than a woman opens the door of the building and waves us inside. She's tall with glasses and curly, mousey brown hair. It's obvious she wants us to get inside before anyone sees us.

She closes the door behind us and draws the blinds. "Sorry, Detectives, but your presence here is awful for business."

I want to tell her too bad, but I need her cooperation so I decide to play nice. "We appreciate your help in this case."

"Yes, well, if you're going to need to look around, I'd appreciate it if you could use the utmost discretion."

Mitchell laughs. "What do you want us to do, pretend Piper and I are here to plan our wedding?"

Miriam nods. "That's exactly what I want you to do."

Mitchell and I exchange awkward looks. Pretending to be his fiancée might be more difficult than finding Loralei McNamara.

CHAPTER SIX

"I guess that makes me the father of the bride," Dad says, wrapping an arm around my shoulders.

"You're hysterical. Really." I take a seat at Miriam's desk. "Mr. McNamara said you had a list of the wedding guests for us."

"Yes." Miriam walks over to the printer behind her desk and removes a paper from the tray. "I just printed it for you." She hands it to me.

I close my eyes for a moment and then read the list of names. Not a one jumps out at me. "Is this everyone?" I ask.

"Everyone except the wedding party. They're on the seating chart. One moment." She presses a few keys on her computer, and the printer starts up again. Once it's finished, she hands that paper to me.

Almost immediately, a name jumps out at me, along with the saying "Something borrowed, something blue." "Who is Catherine Ellis?"

Miriam is on her computer again. "She was the maid of honor. Why?"

Mitchell and Dad are both looking at me. "Is she from out of town?" I ask.

"Yes. She lives in Chatam, New Jersey."

Mitchell has his notepad out and is scribbling Catherine's information.

"I'd like to see the room where the bride and her wedding party got ready."

Miriam sighs, like she was afraid I was going to say that. Her eyes go to Mitchell's badge on a chain around his neck. "I'll need you to put your badge somewhere less visible. And"—she motions between us—"if you two could hold hands or link arms or something to play the part of the happily engaged couple, I would greatly appreciate it."

Dad stifles a laugh next to me, and I shoot him a glare. "Come on, pumpkin. Let's go plan your wedding."

I stand up and place the seating chart and guest list in my purse. "You are enjoying this way too much." Of course, he probably suspects we'll never do this for real since I've never shown any interest in settling down with anyone. It's not in the cards for me. No man would want his entire life on display every time his wife touched him. It's too intimate, and given that most people don't want their spouses to be privy to their every thought—the divorce rate would be much higher if that were the case—I'm destined to live alone.

When we reach the door, Miriam's eyes widen at Mitchell and me, and she blocks our exit. Mitchell's badge is now under his jacket, so I'm not sure what the issue is. When neither of us moves, she motions back and forth between our hands.

Mitchell extends his hand to me, but there's no way I'm holding his hand. Especially when it would be my right hand. Who knows what I'd read off of him? He might be the type to hook up with bridesmaids in the bathroom. I do not want to see that. I walk around him and loop my left arm through his.

"This is as good as it gets," I tell Miriam.

She scowls but opens the door.

Since it's still early in the day, there aren't many people around. She walks us along the pathways, which are made with stones that look like they belong in fine jewelry not in the ground for people to walk on.

"It's this building over here," Miriam says. "They booked the largest ballroom to accommodate the lengthy guest list."

There are two hundred names on the guest list, so I assumed the ballroom would be quite large. When we approach, I notice the wooden double doors are etched with roses.

"This room is called the Rose Gardens," Miriam says, opening the door for us.

My jaw nearly drops when I see the inside of the ballroom. There's a red carpet in the entranceway leading down a hallway to a huge room filled with tables with white linens. There is a grand piano in the far corner beyond the cherry wood dance floor. Over the dance floor, an enormous crystal chandelier hangs from the ceiling. Beyond that is a stage for a live band. In the opposite direction is a stone fountain surrounded by vases, which are currently empty. Next to the fountain is a long table, which I know from the seating chart is where the wedding party sat.

"The bridal room is this way," Miriam says, leading us across the room to one of two doors.

"What's the other door?" Mitchell asks, making me realize I'm still holding his arm even though there is no chance of anyone seeing us in here. I quickly drop my arm.

"That would be were the groom and his groomsmen got ready."

She opens the door to the bridal room. I'd love to get a read on the room without Miriam watching since she has no idea what I do for a living. She thinks we're all police detectives, and I prefer it that way. I don't need her judgmental stares.

Dad must sense my unease because he says, "Ms. King, would it be possible for you to show me the groom's room while my partners check the bridal room? That way we could get out of your hair quicker."

Miriam looks torn between not keeping an eye on us all and wanting us gone, but she relents. "I suppose so." She leads Dad to the other room, and I mouth a silent thank you.

Mitchell and I step into the bridal room, and I walk over to the red upholstered chairs. There are ten of them in all, but there's no way for me to figure out which one Loralei sat in. I move toward the vanity, assuming Loralei would have sat there. I take a seat and look into the mirror.

"Picturing yourself in a veil?" Mitchell asks, standing behind me.

"Hardly. I'm trying to get a read on anything Loralei might have used." I press my hand to the top surface of the vanity. Nothing. "Twice today, the expression 'Something borrowed, something blue' has popped into my head. I don't know what to make of it."

"Isn't that part of the tradition where the bridesmaids give the bride gifts and they have to be things that are old, new, borrowed, and blue?"

I raise my eyes to his reflection in the mirror. "And you know about that because…"

He shoves his hands into his pockets. "It's in enough movies that most people know about it."

"You mean you don't frequent weddings in the hopes of picking up single bridesmaids?"

He cocks his head. "Is that why you wouldn't hold my hand?"

He's getting to know me too well. I clear my throat. "Back to the case. I heard that expression in my head when I saw Catherine Ellis's name on the seating chart. She's connected to this in some way."

"Do you think she gave Loralei something borrowed and blue?"

I nod. "But what, and why is it important?" I open the vanity drawer. Inside is a small hand mirror, I suppose to use in conjunction with the vanity mirror to see the back of your hair. There's also a pack of breath mints, a four-sided nail file, a brush, tissues, and, in the event of the unlucky bride, feminine hygiene products. I shut the drawer again since all the items are brand new and have obviously been replaced since Loralei's wedding.

I stand up and walk around Mitchell to the patio doors on the other side of the room. I push the curtain aside to look out at the lawn area. With the curtain gripped in my right hand, I get the familiar tingle of a vision.

"Why would you give me this, Catherine? I don't even know how I'm supposed to react to it." Loralei is gazing outside, tears filling her eyes.

"You need a garter, right? Every bride wears one."

"But it was hers. *She wore it when she married Elijah."*

"So what? They got divorced months later. It's completely meaningless. And now you're marrying Steven. It's water under the bridge."

"Do you have any idea what you're saying? Elijah is the last person I need to think about on my wedding day."

"Maybe so, but we both know you were already thinking

46

about him. I remember how much you cried when he married Mindy. You practically begged me to go to their wedding so I could tell you all about it. It was sadistic, Lor, but I did it because you asked me to, and then I caught the damn garter."

"I don't want it. I don't want anything of hers."

"But you want him. Admit it. You still want him."

Tears choke Loralei, reducing her to a blubbering mess.

I open my eyes to find I'm in Mitchell's arms.

"That must have been a hell of a vision," he says, wiping my wet cheeks with his sleeve.

"Don't." I push out of his arms and stand up. The hollow ache in my chest is too much. This is awful. "God, why do people do this to themselves?"

"Do what? Piper, you haven't told me what you saw."

"I was right about Elijah. She was still in love with him."

His eyes become mere slits. "But you said he wasn't the one who kidnapped her. You thought he was telling the truth about not having seen her in years."

"He's hiding something. She couldn't still be this much in love with him if they never even spoke." I press my palm against my chest to keep it from shattering.

"So you think they were in contact, but they didn't physically see each other?" He exhales loudly. "That doesn't seem to fit the MO for the relationship they had in high school. That was *all* physical, wasn't it?"

"Maybe on his end, but she was in love with him." The pain tearing through me is unbearable.

"Stop that. You look like you're trying to crush your chest." Mitchell reaches for my hand, but I turn slightly away from him.

"I'm trying to stop my chest from caving in."

"By pushing on it?" Mitchell raises a brow at me in challenge. "You're smarter than that, Piper. Besides, you're the one who told me the pain you feel from visions isn't real."

It's not the result of physical trauma, but it sure as hell feels real. "I'd like to see you try to tell yourself this isn't real." I rub the heel of my hand in a circle above my heart. This is just further proof that I have no intention of getting close enough to any man to experience this heartache firsthand.

"Do we go back to Elijah, or do you want to eat a gallon of ice cream and watch Lifetime movies for the rest of the day?" The corner of his mouth curves up ever so slightly.

"Right now I'm thinking about making my own Lifetime movie about the psychic PI who goes psycho on her partner's ass."

Mitchell twists around to check out his backside. "It's too nice an ass to ruin. You'd never go through with it."

"I'm glad you think so, but I regret to inform you I don't share your obsession with your body." I'm pretty much alone in that, too. Most women fawn all over Mitchell. And while I have gotten a good view of his ass when he pressed it up against my car window when I refused to talk to him, I'm not going to throw myself at him any time soon. Or ever.

"You two about ready to go?" Dad asks, walking into the bridal room.

I wipe a stray tear from my left eye and move past him out the door. "I should check the groom's room as well. Just in case there's anything you didn't pick up on." I know Dad will decipher my cryptic speech, but Miriam will be in the dark.

"You are more perceptive than I am," Dad says. "Though I suppose I should look around in here to make sure you two didn't miss anything. All part of the procedure," Dad tells Miriam, who has her arms crossed and an annoyed look on her face. We're clearly taking too long for her liking.

I step into the groom's room, which is set up much like the bridal room. The difference is that instead of a vanity, there's a small bar.

"Sweet," Mitchell says, walking over to the bar and picking up a bottle of vodka.

"You're on duty," I remind him.

"I wasn't planning on indulging in any. I just think it's nice that they provide a bar for anyone who might be getting cold feet."

"So you think people should get drunk and marry someone they have reservations about spending their lives with?"

"I never said anything about getting drunk. Just a healthy buzz to ease the nerves." He shrugs and places the bottle of vodka back on the bar.

I don't respond to his comment because it's moot in this case anyway. Steven wanted to marry Loralei. He was eager to do it.

"Maybe you should have a drink." He picks up the bottle and thrusts it toward me.

"I don't—" I can feel a familiar energy coming from the bottle. I take it in my hand and clear my mind, allowing the energy to flow to me.

"What if she doesn't show?" Steven says before pouring a glass of vodka and downing it.

"Her parents love you. Don't sweat it. She'll be there with her father walking her down the aisle to you, and then she's all yours. No worries." The shorter man places his hand on Steven's shoulder and squeezes it.

I don't see anything else, so I put the bottle down on the

bar. "Steven was worried Loralei wouldn't show for the wedding," I tell Mitchell.

"That sounds about right."

It doesn't help us, though, because it doesn't offer any information we didn't already know. "This was a dead end," I say. "We might as well get out of here."

"Detectives," Miriam says, walking into the room with Dad in tow. "I have another appointment in just a few minutes. We really need to wrap this up." She twirls a finger in the air as if that will emphasize her point.

"We're finished here," I say. "Thank you very much for your cooperation, Ms. King."

She nods, and her gaze is locked on Mitchell and me. "Until you are off the premises, I'd appreciate it if you two kept up the ruse of being engaged."

I roll my eyes as I loop my left arm through Mitchell's.

He flexes his bicep and smiles at me. "You could do worse," he says.

"I could do so much better, though."

Miriam huffs, turns on her heel, and walks out of the ballroom. She doesn't bother to say goodbye when we reach the parking lot in front of her office.

"She's pleasant," I say, opening the car door and getting inside.

"She wasn't wearing a wedding ring," Mitchell says. "It's a classic situation of the bitter middle-aged woman who plans weddings for happy couples and can't find love herself." He starts the car and pulls out of the lot.

"Were you checking her finger for a ring because you wanted to see if you could hook up with the wedding planner?" I ask.

"Do you two ever give it a rest?" Dad asks. "I can't figure

you out. One minute you're at each other's throats and the next you're having sleepovers."

"We don't have sleepovers, Dad. We work through the night sometimes." Truth be told, we have slept over each other's places, but it was after I'd had mind-numbing visions that completely incapacitated me, and Mitchell was feeling the need to protect me—or more accurately, make up for not protecting his mother.

"Banter is our thing," Mitchell says. "It helps us focus."

"Sure." Dad's sarcasm isn't lost on either of us.

Mitchell pulls up to my office and leaves the car idling. "I need to check in at the station. I'll meet you guys later, okay?"

"It's family dinner night. Why don't you meet Piper and me there?" Dad says.

Mitchell smiles. "I'm not going to turn down a home-cooked meal. Can I bring anything?"

"A bottle of wine. I may need it to get through dinner with you two." Dad shuts the car door and follows me into the office. The new desk is set up next to mine, and the spare office key is sitting on top of it with a note from Marcia.

Piper,

All went well with the delivery. Here's the key and a copy of the delivery slip.

Marcia

"Nice, Dad," I say, running my hand over the surface of the cherry wood desk. "Did you have to get a desk that dwarfs mine?"

He shrugs. "I'm older than you are. I need a comfortable desk and chair."

I sit down in his chair, which has leather so soft it feels like butter. "You've got to be kidding me."

Dad motions for me to get up. "My turn. You have your own desk."

I stand up and grab the delivery slip. I feel a familiar tingle of energy, and when I scan the paper, one of the deliverymen's names pops out at me. *Joel Underwood.*

"Piper?" Dad asks, knowing the look on my face all too well. "What did you see?"

I point to the name. "I need you to look into this Joel Underwood. He's connected to the case somehow."

CHAPTER SEVEN

I spend the rest of the day finishing up with the background check while Dad looks into this Joel Underwood person and calls Mitchell to fill him in. Something seems off to me about Joel's name popping up. Why would anyone connected to the case also be delivering furniture to my office? It just doesn't make sense. The sign on my door would let them know about my abilities, so why would this guy risk coming into contact with me if he did something wrong?

Unless he didn't do anything wrong. Maybe he's connected to Loralei in some other way. Maybe he offered to help her run away because he's a friend of hers and didn't want to see her stuck in a loveless marriage. I rub my forehead, trying to will my mind to make sense of this.

Dad hangs up his phone, laying it atop his desk. "Well, Mitchell didn't find anything in the system for this guy. He's clean. I also called Steven McNamara, and he has no idea who this person is or what connection he could have to Loralei."

Some days—okay, every day—I wish my visions were

clearer. They seem to come in pieces. "Whispers" is the word I like to use for them. Faint whispers of information I have to piece together before someone winds up dead. It's not a fun game to play.

I stand up and grab my jacket off the back of my chair. "Let's go to dinner. You know Mom hates it when we're late and the food starts to get cold."

Dad jumps to his feet. "You don't know the half of it. The lecture doesn't stop when you leave."

I laugh as we exit the office, and I lock up for the night.

Mitchell's Explorer is already at the house when we arrive. Dad and I exchange a look when we walk in to find Mitchell in an apron, helping Mom cook.

I hang my coat in the hall closet and step into the kitchen. "I didn't know you were the Betty Crocker type," I say, leaning against the counter and looking him up and down in Mom's floral apron.

"Leave him alone. I needed an extra hand, and since you and your father are late, Mitchell graciously volunteered to help out. I wasn't going to let him get his nice shirt and pants splattered with sauce." She removes the garlic bread from the oven and places it on the stove.

I grab a wicker basket, line it with a napkin, and start breaking the bread apart at the premade cuts she made. "Did you make sausage and meatballs?"

"Well, technically, *I* made the meatballs," Mitchell says, stirring the pot of sauce.

"Exactly how long have you been here?"

"Forty-five minutes or so." He turns off the heat on the stovetop and begins ladling the sauce into a big serving bowl. "What took you guys so long?"

"We were working. Imagine that." I bring the garlic bread to the dining room table, which Mom has already set.

There are two bottles of wine in the center of the table, one red and one white. I immediately pour myself a glass of red and take a healthy sip.

"Is there any chance this Joel guy is popping up on your radar for another reason?" Mitchell asks, setting the bowl of sauce down on the table.

"I suppose." It's not like I haven't gotten visions of different crimes at the same time before. The worst is when they overlap in what seems like the same vision.

"Maybe you need to learn to read between the crimes," Mitchell says with a smirk.

I roll my eyes. "Worst attempt at a joke ever."

His expression suddenly goes serious. "Do you ever...?" He looks down at the green tablecloth. "Are your visions ever of the future?"

"I typically see things that have already happened or that are happening now." I've been working on tapping into my third eye more and triggering some clairvoyant visions, but it's been a slow process and nothing I truly trust yet. So far the only things I've managed to see before they happen are a baseball player hitting a homerun and me dropping a glass in the sink and it shattering.

Mitchell inhales deeply. I know he's thinking about his mother, who was clearly a gifted clairvoyant. We could use her ability right about now, but I'm the best we have. I place my left hand on his arm in an attempt at a comforting gesture, but he immediately checks to make sure I'm not trying to read him. He relaxes when he sees it's my left hand on his arm.

Still, I lower my hand to my side. "I said I wouldn't try to read you anymore."

"I know." He shakes his head. "It's just when I think about her—"

55

"Dinner is served," Mom says, bringing the baked ziti into the dining room.

Mitchell and I take our seats, the conversation over since he doesn't talk about his mother with anyone but me. Dad gives us a knowing look. I might be the psychic, but I've always suspected Dad has a sixth sense as well. He just doesn't know how to tune into it properly.

"Your father told me his desk is nearly twice the size of yours," Mom says, serving the ziti. She gives Dad an admonishing glare. "When I helped him pick out that desk, I told him it came in two sizes and he should choose accordingly."

"I did. The office has plenty of space for that desk." Dad takes his plate from Mom and grabs some garlic bread.

"Yeah, and there's still plenty of room for a client to huddle against the wall," I say.

"Standing room only." Mitchell laughs. "I'm sorry I missed seeing your face when you saw the desk."

"You laugh now, but it's going to be you standing in the corner."

"You're exaggerating," Dad says. "We each have chairs on the opposite sides of our desks. There's plenty of space for clients."

"More space at *his* desk though, right?" Mitchell whispers, nudging my arm with his elbow.

"This is nice," Mom says. "I miss entertaining guests." She smiles at Mitchell. One of these days, she's going to get it out of her head that there's any kind of future for Mitchell and me other than a professional relationship.

Mom hates work talk at the dinner table, so we discuss other things until everyone is finished eating.

"Thank you, Mrs. Ashwell. That was delicious," Mitchell says.

"Thank you for your help."

"Speaking of," I say, "Mitchell, why don't you help me load the dishwasher?"

He stands up and grabs his plate and Mom's. I take mine and Dad's.

"You two sit and relax. We've got this," I tell them.

Mom gives me a sly smile around her wineglass, which I choose to ignore as I walk into the kitchen.

"I really like your mom," Mitchell says, rinsing the plates in the sink.

I open the dishwasher and wait for him to hand me the plates. "She's great. A tad meddlesome, though."

He laughs. "You should have heard the stuff she told me about you before you got here." He hands me a plate.

"What kind of stuff?"

"Oh, you know, about how you never date."

I shove the plate into an open slot in the dishwasher. "I'm sure you responded with how often you do date."

"Actually, I haven't been on a date in a while. Not since the Veronica Castell case."

He hasn't dated since our last case? "Why is that? Are you losing your charm? Or are women finally realizing you never had any?"

He smirks. "Not sure. Maybe it's that I'm afraid working in close proximity to you will show you more of me than I'm comfortable with."

"Ah. Performance issues or are you afraid I'll laugh if I see you naked?"

He hands me some silverware and leans closer. "I can assure you I have no performance issues, nor am I bashful about what I look like naked."

I take the silverware and turn away from him. Neither is something I can think about—in relation to him or any man. "I take it you're one of those people who likes to take selfies and stare at their reflection. What I've come to discover is those people are usually more delusional than the rest of us."

He turns off the faucet and dries his hands, all while studying my face in a way that makes me want to turn and run away. "When are you going to admit you're attracted to me?"

I scoff. "I can't admit what isn't true." Is he good-looking? Yes. I'd have to be blind not to notice that. But am I attracted to him? Ludicrous.

"What were you saying about delusional people?" He raises a brow at me and walks back into the dining room.

———

Equipped with coffee and muffins from Marcia's Café, Dad, Mitchell, and I stare at each other in my office for a good twenty minutes on Wednesday morning. We've got nothing to go on. Joel Underwood seems clean, but I still want to meet him in person so I can get a good read on him. Maybe that's our next move since we aren't getting any other leads on Loralei's disappearance.

I look up Joel, but the search doesn't yield an address other than a PO box. I pull up the delivery company he works for and put the address into the navigation on my phone. "Anyone up for a field trip to Triumph Deliveries?" I ask, standing up.

"Time to check out Joel?" Dad asks.

"He didn't come up in the system, Piper. The guy is clean," Mitchell protests.

"Just because he hasn't been caught committing a crime doesn't mean he hasn't committed one." I start for the door, my car keys in hand.

Dad and Mitchell follow, and we get into my Mazda. I don't acknowledge the look they share. They've made it clear they don't like when I drive while on a case like this. If I get a vision, it could be dangerous for all of us. But since I don't have anything but a name to go on, the likelihood of me having a vision in my own car is close to nonexistent. I've become very good at blocking energy unless I'm trying to read it.

Triumph Deliveries is a warehouse on Temple Street. I park in front, and we walk inside in what I hope looks like an intimidating trio. This section of town is on the outskirts and nothing like the rest of Weltunkin. In fact, most people don't even realize it still is considered within the Weltunkin borders. Mitchell approaches the first person we see, who happens to be a woman in her late twenties with strawberry blonde hair and dimples that make an appearance when Mitchell smiles at her. I roll my eyes, still not used to the way women react to him.

"Good morning," Mitchell says, his voice slightly deeper than usual. *Good Lord, help us all.* "I was wondering if you'd be able to help us. I'm Detective Mitchell Brennan with the Weltunkin PD, and these are my partners." He gestures to us with a sweeping motion of his hand but doesn't bother to introduce us by name. "We're looking for a Joel Underwood. Does he happen to be here now?"

The woman's face is flushed, and she's smiling like a schoolgirl crushing on the popular boy. It's enough to make me sick. She flips through some papers on the clipboard she's carrying. "You're in luck. Joel isn't scheduled to leave until ten. You'll find him in the loading area." She clasps the clipboard to her chest and bats her eyelashes at Mitchell. "I'd be happy to walk you back there if you'd like."

"I would love that," Mitchell says, laying it on thick and

topping it off with extending the crook of his arm for her to take.

Dad eyes me with an odd expression on his face.

"What?" I mouth, but he doesn't respond.

We follow Mitchell and his new plaything to the loading dock, and I don't need anyone to point out Joel to me. I know who he is the minute I see him. I step past Mitchell and the woman and walk right over to Joel, who is loading boxes into the back of his truck. He's about thirty with thinning hair and a small moustache. He's also barely taller than I am, which I'm assuming puts him at five foot six.

"Joel Underwood?" I say even though I already know it's him.

"Who's asking?" He stops what he's doing and faces me. His face softens as he takes in my body from head to toe. I will my abilities not to tune in on what he's thinking right now or what kind of perverted thoughts he's had in the past.

"I'm Piper Ashwell. I'm a private investigator working with the Weltunkin PD to solve a missing persons case. I need to ask you a few questions." I extend my hand to him while clearing my mind.

He gives me an odd look but takes my hand.

"When are you going to get a place of your own? You don't even pay rent. Your father and I can't afford to keep paying for your food and all your bills. We're retired, Joel. It's time you grow up and act like an adult for once."

When I don't let go of Joel's hand he steps toward me. "I get off work around—"

Mitchell pulls my hand from Joel's and steps between us. He flashes his badge in Joel's face. "Detective Brennan." Once Joel breaks the staring contest he's started with me and acknowledges the badge, Mitchell lowers it so it falls in front of his chest on the chain he likes to wear. "How do you know Loralei McNamara?"

Joel's face scrunches up in confusion. "I've never heard of her."

"What about Loralei Allen? That was her maiden name."

Joel holds up his hands. "Look, I don't know anyone named Loralei. Did I deliver a package to her or something? Because if it was damaged, she needs to call—"

"Like Ms. Ashwell said, we're investigating a missing person. This has nothing to do with your deliveries." Mitchell is still partially blocking my view of Joel.

I step to the side and look Joel in the eyes. He's telling the truth. He doesn't know Loralei. So why did his name pop up as connected to the case?

"Let's go. He doesn't know anything," I say, spinning on my heel and starting for the door.

Behind me, Mitchell says, "Here's my card. If you remember Loralei at all, give me a call."

"I'll check my delivery schedule to see if she was on it at any point. If she turns up, I'll let you know," Joel says.

Mitchell and Dad catch up with me at my car.

"What did you see?" Dad asks me.

"Nothing really. He's living off his parents. This guy has nothing going for him, and I got the sense he was telling the truth about not knowing Lorelei." I start the engine and grip the steering wheel tightly.

"Then why did you see his name?" Mitchell asks. "Have your abilities ever led you in the wrong direction?"

I don't bother to pull out of the parking spot because I don't know where to go next. I lean my head back on the headrest. "No. What I sense is always important. It means I'm misinterpreting it."

Mitchell leans forward from the back seat. "Maybe you should look at the delivery slip again."

I let out a deep, frustrated sigh, and Mitchell puts his hand on my shoulder.

"You'll get this, Piper. You will."

"Is it possible you saw Joel's name for another reason?" Dad asks. "Maybe it's not connected to Loralei at all."

"Talk us through it," Mitchell suggests, his hand still on my shoulder.

"All I saw was his mother complaining that she and his father still pay all his bills."

Mitchell rubs the five o'clock shadow on his chin. "What if...?" He pauses, and I see him working through the mental battle taking place in his mind. "Is it possible he's living with his parents and not listing a physical address anywhere because he's doing something illegal like not paying his taxes."

"Tax evasion." The words come off my lips with that definitive truth I know well. "That's it. He's guilty of tax evasion." I slam my open palm against the steering wheel. This has nothing to do with Loralei's case. "I should have done a better job at blocking things that weren't connected to her."

"This isn't your fault, Piper," Mitchell says.

"He's right, pumpkin. You can't control what you see."

Maybe not, but I just sent us on a wild goose chase that cost us time and might be costing Loralei a lot more.

CHAPTER EIGHT

Thanks to my latest discovery about Joel Underwood, Mitchell's afternoon is tied up with the IRS and proving Joel is guilty of tax evasion. I'm sensing jail time in Joel's future. At least that will get him out of his parents' house.

I spend the rest of the day in my office, working smaller cases. Dad is researching Loralei online, checking all her social media accounts to see the last time she posted anywhere. I take his silence to mean she hasn't. She's gone off the grid.

"Piper, could you please stop tapping your pen against your desk? It's driving me batty," Dad says.

"Sorry." I still the pen. The truth is, the repetitious thudding of the pen was helping me focus. "I think I need to go for a walk to clear my head."

"Tell Marcia I said hi and grab me a cup of coffee while you're there." Dad doesn't look up from his laptop, but the corner of his mouth tips up in a smile. He knows me well.

It's unusually warm today, so I leave my jacket draped over the back of my chair and walk the twenty-three steps to Marcia's Nook. The bell above the door announces my arrival. Story time is going on in the children's section, so I creep past the moms bobbing toddlers on their laps in an attempt to keep them quiet for the story. Marcia is reading today, which means her usual story time reader must have called out. She smiles at me as I head straight for the mystery section in the back.

I scan the titles, looking for anything about missing persons. Sometimes reading about cases like the ones I'm working helps me figure things out. Once, it even spurred a vision because the case was so similar to the one I was working on. I settle on a book titled *The Missing Girl.* Since Marcia is busy at the moment and there's no one working the register, I plop down in one of the comfy reading chairs in the corner and open the book.

Thirty minutes later, I'm a few chapters into the book, which is nothing like the case I'm working on, but I believe in finishing a book once I start it, so I take it to the register where Marcia is ringing up purchases, mostly of the picture books she read during story hour. I check my phone for any messages from Dad or Mitchell. None. This case is one dead end after another.

First Elijah, then the wedding reception, and finally Joel Underwood. None of these supposed leads gave me anything to work with.

"Piper?" Marcia says.

I blink my eyes to clear the fog that's descended upon me. The line in front of me is gone, so I step up to the counter with my book. "Sorry."

"Rough day?" Marcia starts getting me a coffee even though I didn't ask for one.

"Seems to be the norm for me lately. Oh, I need a regular roast for my dad, too."

"None for Mitchell?" she asks. I often suspect she'd be

interested in Mitchell if not for my professional connection to him.

"No, he's at the station. It's just me and my dad right now."

"You sound disappointed." She places my toasted almond on the counter and sets to work pouring Dad's coffee.

"It's just that my visions aren't seeming to help with this case."

"Well, that doesn't seem right at all." She caps Dad's coffee, and instead of ringing me up, she leans on the counter. "Tell me what you've got so far."

I give her an abridged version of my visions. Sure, she's not a detective and she's not actually working this case in any capacity, but she's my only real friend and there's no way Steven McNamara is going to find out I've shared information with her.

"So you're seeing two different cases at the same time? That's nothing new, right?"

"Not common but definitely not new," I say.

"Unless..." She dips her head to the right and then the left as if mentally weighing her thoughts.

"Unless what?" I ask.

"Well, is it possible they are connected but not in the way you'd think?"

"Like Loralei was evading her taxes, too?" I ask. Nothing comes to me as fact, so I know that's not right.

"Or the person who kidnapped her was." She stands up straight and shrugs. "What do I know? I'm fascinated by what you do, but I can't make heads or tails of it. Sorry." She starts ringing me up.

My vision from the wedding had to do with Mindy Thomas, Elijah's ex-wife. What if she is mixed up in a tax evasion scheme of some sort? She could also be connected to Loralei's kidnapping. It's possible there's a connection there, and there's only one way to find out. I need to talk to her. Or better yet, I need to talk to Elijah again first. "Actually, Marcia, I think what you said might be very helpful after all." I use my phone to pay and grab the coffees and book, balancing the book in the crook of my arm. "Thanks."

"Happy to help," she says as I push my back against the door and head to my office.

The second I'm inside my office, I tell Dad, "Suit up. We're heading back to Elijah's."

He looks up from his laptop. "Did you have a vision?"

"No, but Marcia helped me realize something about my visions. Come on. We'll call Mitchell and tell him to meet us there."

While Dad drives, I call Mitchell and fill both him and Dad in on the theory I've put together so we're all on the same page when we pull up to Elijah's place. He opens the door and sighs when he sees us.

"I've already told you everything," Elijah says, leaning his head against the door. But I'm convinced that isn't true. I think he offered to let me read him again the last time we were here because he was hoping his compliance would keep me from taking him up on the offer. He didn't think I'd call his bluff. Unfortunately for me, he was right.

"How is it you're always home during the day?" Mitchell asks.

"I work from home most days."

"Doing what exactly?" Mitchell presses.

"I'm a headhunter. How is this related to your case?" His impatience with us is only making me want to get inside that house more.

"Mr. Graham, we'd like to talk to you about your ex-wife, not Loralei."

Elijah jerks his head up. "Mindy? Why?"

I'm not about to tell him the real reason while standing on his front porch. "May we come inside to speak to you in a more private setting, please?"

He huffs but steps aside.

His place is a mess. The coffee table is littered with empty pizza boxes and dirty napkins. My guess is he hasn't left the house since we were here last and he's been living off of delivery. I pick up a discarded sweatshirt on the couch so I can sit, and Elijah quickly grabs it from me.

"What can you tell us about your ex-wife?" Dad asks, sitting beside me while Mitchell opts to stand.

Elijah scoffs like he's trying to get a bad taste out of his mouth. "She divorced me and took me for every penny. That's why I had to leave Weltunkin and move into this place. It was a foreclosure, but it's all I can afford. I'm broke thanks to that bitch. Her and her stupid alimony checks." It's clear he's speaking the truth. His hatred for Mindy is evident in his rigid posture and gritted teeth.

"Mr. Graham, do you have anything that belonged to Mindy?" I ask.

"Why?"

I want to get a read on her. She has to have some significance to this case, or I wouldn't have had a vision about her. "I think she's connected to all of this somehow."

"What, you think Mindy kidnapped Loralei? That's crazy."

"Did Mindy know about your relationship with Loralei?" Mitchell asks.

"Look, we talked, okay? But that was it. Loralei wanted more than I was willing to give. I tried to let her down easy.

It wasn't like I was screwing her anymore. Mindy had no reason to hate Loralei."

"Even so, if you have anything of Mindy's, I'd like to see it." I could picture Mindy getting upset when she found out Loralei was still pining over her husband. It would be even worse if she knew Loralei had her garter. I don't think Mindy would hurt Loralei, but kidnapping her to teach her a lesson is a different story. She even could have hired someone to do it for her.

"I don't understand how seeing something of Mindy's would help. You're supposedly psychic. Why can't you just *see*"—he makes air quotes—"what you need to?"

"Mocking what I do isn't helping you, Mr. Graham." I've encountered more skeptics than believers, so his reaction to my abilities isn't anything new. "You keep claiming you're innocent in all this, but you're clearly hiding something or you'd direct us to any of Mindy's belongings you still possess."

Elijah lets out a puff of air and runs a hand through his dark hair. "The only thing I'm hiding is that I kept in touch with Loralei. We'd hook up every once in a while. It was no big deal. But then she stopped calling me. It was right around the time I met Mindy, so there's no connection between Mindy and Lor. I don't know why she stopped reaching out to me. I didn't really care either because like I said, it was always just a physical thing between us."

The fact that Mindy came along at the same time Loralei stopped calling Elijah makes me want to see Mindy's things even more. And the fact that Elijah just referred to her as "Lor" instead of Loralei tells me they were closer than he's admitting. "What you just said leads me to believe your ex-wife did know about Loralei. Now, I'm going to ask one more time. Do you have anything of Mindy's here at the house?"

"I guess I can check to see if she left anything behind. Can I get back to you about it?"

I know damn well if we leave, we aren't going to hear from Elijah again. He doesn't want anything to do with his ex-wife or this case. "We can wait," I say, leaning back on the couch so he knows we aren't leaving without something of Mindy's.

He doesn't even attempt to mask his eye roll before turning and walking to the hall closet. He seems to know exactly what he's looking for, despite telling us he'd have to see if she left anything behind. He opens the closet door and retrieves a white garment bag, a lot like the one Loralei's wedding dress was in.

I stand up and walk over to him with Mitchell at my side. "You have her wedding dress?" I can sense the energy coming off it. "She didn't have it cleaned, did she?"

"No. She said she didn't see the point since she'd never wear the thing again. She only kept it because I told her to. I thought one day she might want it." He lets out a sad laugh. "So much for that."

"May I?" I ask, reaching for the garment bag.

"You can keep it," Elijah says. "If you don't, I'll probably wind up burning it."

I unzip the bag, taking deep breaths to clear my mind. The energy coming off this dress is overwhelming. I don't even think I need to touch it to read the memories it contains.

"You okay?" Mitchell asks.

I give a slight nod as Dad places his hand on the small of my back as if to steady me. I close my eyes and count to ten before reaching inside to touch the dress.

Mindy and Elijah are standing in front of a photographer with their entire wedding party, which consists of three women and three men.

"Why did you invite her here?" Mindy whispers between smiles for the camera.

"What's the big deal?" Elijah whispers back.

"What's the big deal? She's her best friend." The smile doesn't return to Mindy's face.

"I haven't seen Loralei in a year."

The maid of honor and best man are both looking at Elijah and Mindy now, aware there's a fight going on.

"I need the happy couple to show how happy they are," the photographer says, eyeing them over the camera.

Mindy plasters a fake smile on her face. Elijah tries and fails to do the same.

"I've done everything you've asked me to. Why are you picking a fight on our wedding day?" Elijah whispers.

"I'm not the one who invited an ex's best friend to our wedding, Elijah."

"Okay, I think we are finished here," the photographer says. "Thank you, everyone."

I blink my eyes into focus. "You lied, Mr. Graham."

Mitchell takes a step closer to Elijah. "Mindy knew all about Loralei, even after you supposedly stopped seeing her. You fought about her on your wedding day."

Elijah holds up his hands. "That was all Mindy's fault. Not mine. So what if I invited a friend Loralei and I have in common? It didn't mean anything."

"You told Mindy you did everything she asked you to do. What did you mean?" I ask.

Elijah runs his hand through his already messy hair. "Fine. I stopped talking to Loralei because Mindy asked me to. She said she wouldn't see me if I didn't commit fully to her. It was Mindy's idea to get married less than a year after we met. I think she thought if we got married..."

"You'd stop cheating on her?" Mitchell asks.

"I didn't cheat on her."

"Not physically," I say. "But you were still in touch with Loralei." I can sense it. The waves of betrayal coming off the dress nearly knock me off my feet. "You *did* love her, didn't you?"

"Of course I loved my wife."

"No. You were in love with Loralei." I turn and look at the disheveled house. "That's why you're such a mess right now. This place didn't look like this until after we told you about Loralei's disappearance. You're devastated that she's missing because you've been in love with her for years."

"So in love that maybe you stopped her from going on her honeymoon?" Mitchell asks, moving closer still to Elijah.

"No! You think I kidnapped her?"

"Or maybe you helped her run away. Maybe you both planned this together. You're divorced now. Mindy is out of the picture. You and Loralei could have staged this kidnapping and she's off somewhere waiting for you."

Something about Mitchell's words sends warning bells off in my head. "Mindy's out of the picture," I repeat, squeezing the dress in my hands. No vision comes this time. Only whispers. Sounds. Feelings.

Fear. Intense fear.

"Why are you doing this? Please. You don't have to do this." Mindy's voice is panicked. And then she screams.

CHAPTER NINE

When I come to, I'm in Mitchell's arms on the floor of Elijah's living room. Dad has Elijah by the arm and looks ready to read him his rights even though he's now retired from the police force.

"You were screaming," Mitchell says.

"Mindy was screaming," I say, looking at Elijah as I sit up with Mitchell's help. "When was the last time you saw your ex-wife?"

"Not since the divorce papers were signed."

"When was that?" I ask, back on my feet.

"About a month ago. Why? What did you see?"

Now he believes in my visions?

"Are you worried about what she might have seen?" Mitchell asks. "Is there anything you'd like to tell us? Or maybe you feel the need to seek legal counsel."

"This is ridiculous," Elijah says. "I didn't do anything to my ex-wife!"

"A few minutes ago you said you wanted to burn her dress," Mitchell says. "Seems like you aren't too fond of her. Why should we believe you now?"

"Piper, what exactly did you see?" Dad asks.

My eyes lock on Elijah, trying to get a read on him. "I think Mindy was pleading for her life, but I didn't see her attacker. I only felt her fear."

"You had goose bumps," Mitchell says.

That means Mindy probably did. I move closer to Elijah. "If you're telling the truth, you won't mind me touching your arm while I ask you a question."

Elijah holds out his arm to me. "Go ahead. If that's what you need to do, be my guest. I didn't hurt Mindy."

I reach for him, although I'm pretty sure he's telling the truth since he's so willing to cooperate after witnessing my visions firsthand.

"Did you harm your ex-wife in any way?" I ask, my right hand on top of his wrist.

"Other than calling her every name in the book for coming between Loralei and me and then walking off with all my money? No. Is there a part of me that hopes that bitch got what she deserves? Yeah." He nods. "If someone did hurt her, I'm sure she deserved it."

I let go of him and turn to Dad. "He's telling the truth." Not that it makes him ex-husband of the year or anything. He pretty much just wished an attack upon his ex-wife. "Mr. Graham, we need Mindy's address. Now."

He narrows his eyes. "You really think she's in trouble?"

"Doesn't look good for you that your ex-wife and your former lover may both be in trouble, now does it?" Mitchell asks, crossing his arms.

"Do I need a lawyer?" Elijah asks me.

"You tell me," I say.

Elijah lets out what sounds like a whimper as he walks past us and slumps down on the couch, burying his face in his hands. "I went to see Loralei."

Mitchell's gaze flicks to me, but I hold up my hand to stop him from doing anything stupid.

"When?" I ask.

"Right before she got married. I begged her not to go through with it. Told her how awful my marriage was and that it was proof she and I were meant to be together." He lifts his head, and tears streak his cheeks. "Yes, I'm in love with her. At first, it was just sex. But after every other relationship I had failed, I realized I wanted more from Loralei. Only I realized it too late. She was already engaged to him. When I told her how I felt, she kicked me out and told me never to contact her again. And I didn't. I swear."

Where's Jezebel? The question pops into my mind. Where is the cute golden retriever? "Mr. Graham, where is your dog?"

His head jerks back at my sudden change in topic. "At the groomer's. Why?"

I don't know why. What made me ask that? "No reason. I just realized she's not here." I shake my head, unsure what to make of that. Something is really off. I'm not sure if Mindy and Loralei's cases are linked or if I'm seeing two separate events. And was Mindy really attacked?

We don't have anything to hold Elijah on, and I have this feeling we need to check up on Mindy as soon as possible.

"We need Mindy's address," I tell him.

"She's living in my house. The one I bought in Weltunkin." He practically spits out the words.

"Your anger toward your ex-wife isn't helping you any," Mitchell says.

"He meant what he said before," I interject. "He wouldn't lose sleep if Mindy was attacked, but he's not behind it." I hand Elijah my phone. "Put the address in my navigation, and we'll get out of your hair."

"For now," Mitchell adds, not convinced Elijah isn't somehow responsible for at least one of the women's predicaments.

Elijah types the address and hands me my phone. "Will you keep me posted on Loralei? I need to know she's okay."

I can't shake this feeling that he'll know if anything happens to Loralei. But why? He didn't know she was missing until we told him. God, these visions are messing with my head. "I'll be in touch," I say, walking toward the door. The wedding dress is on the ground where I must have dropped it during my vision. I bend down to pick it up. "Mr. Graham, I'm going to take you up on your offer of keeping this." There's so much energy pulsating from it I know there are more memories to read.

Elijah just waves a hand in the air and continues to cry.

"Weird that he's so upset," Mitchell says, standing outside his Explorer.

"I was thinking the same," Dad says. "Though if he really does love Loralei, I can see how he'd be scared for her."

"Scared and wanting to help," I say. "Why totally break down and cry?"

"Do you need some downtime?" Dad asks. "I can bring you home. Mitchell and I can check in on Mindy."

"No. I need to go." I get in the passenger seat.

"I'll follow you," Mitchell says since I have the address.

Dad drives us back to Weltunkin. He doesn't ask how I'm doing, but he keeps glancing at me. I lean my head on the cold window glass. It soothes the ache caused by all the visions I've been having. Before I know it, the car is stopped and we're sitting in the driveway of a white colonial in a nice residential area in Weltunkin.

"I can see why Elijah is bitter he lost this place," I say, getting out of the car.

Mitchell's car door slams behind me. "Damn. This place must have at least five bedrooms, judging by the size."

It's nothing compared to the mansion we visited on our last case, but the house is really nice. We walk up to the front door, and Dad rings the bell. I look at the flowerbeds in front of the house while we wait. One group of flowers looks like someone stepped on it. I bend down to examine it.

"What is it?" Dad asks.

"These flowers are crushed."

Dad crouches down next to me. "Maybe someone stepped off the porch and landed on the flowers."

Wrong. I can feel it. It's like a cloudiness that settles over me. "No. Someone was running away."

"Neighborhood kids pulling a prank?" Mitchell asks. "You know, ring the bell and then run away."

Ding dong.

The crunch of stems snapping.

I push the branches aside and see part of a shoe print. "That's exactly what happened. But it wasn't a neighborhood kid or a prank."

"How do you know?" Mitchell asks. "Did you see something?"

"I heard it."

Mitchell peers through the window in the front door. "The etched glass makes it too difficult to see inside. There aren't any lights on, though. My guess is no one is home."

"Because Mindy hasn't been here in days." I stand up and reach for the doorbell.

"Piper, no one is here," Mitchell says, but I press the button anyway.

Gloved hand.

Ding dong.

The crunch of stems snapping.

"They were wearing black gloves. They rang the bell and ran off through the flowerbed." I turn and look in the direction the person must have run. With Dad and Mitchell in tow, I start walking. With each step, I wait for my intuition to tell me if I'm going the right way. I'm not getting anything, though.

I stop at the edge of the house and look in both directions. "Which way did he go?"

"He?" Dad asks. "Are you sure it was a man?"

I nod. The gloved hand definitely belongs to a man.

"Elijah?" Mitchell asks.

My senses don't confirm or deny, so I shrug. I press my hand to the side of the house. Nothing. "Where would he run?" I say, thinking aloud.

"Not to the front because Mindy would see him when she went to the door," Mitchell says.

Yes. He's right. The gloved man went around back. I move toward the backyard, which is fenced in. I reach for the latch on the gate.

Gloved hand.

A slight creak from rusty hinges.

I open the gate, and it creaks exactly like I know it will. "This is where he went."

Dad holds the gate open as I step through. The backyard contains a large patio with a table, chairs, deluxe grill, and bar. The yard itself has a few trees with a large hammock nestled between them, and a giant shed, the size of a small house, is situated in the back corner.

"Where to, Piper?" Mitchell asks.

"I'm not a hound dog," I say. Nothing is jumping out at me. The shed is a miniature version of the house. Identical in almost every way but size. I don't sense anything there, so I don't think this guy is hiding out inside. I turn toward the house. The back deck is large and houses a Jacuzzi.

"Tell me we get to soak in that in hopes of a vision," Mitchell says.

I flash him a reprimanding look as I climb the four steps to the lower deck. Energy comes from the Jacuzzi, but I can tell it isn't related to the man in the gloves, so I move to the sliding glass door.

I reach for the handle and see the gloved hand again.

"Time to pay for what you've done, Mindy. You aren't deserving of the name Graham. And you know the vow you took: 'Til death. So it will be."

CHAPTER TEN

I let go of the handle, my chest heaving.

"Piper?" Dad is beside me with one arm wrapped around my back to steady me.

"I heard his thoughts." My fists clench at my sides as I try to tamp down the anger he felt before attacking her.

"Can you tell us?" Mitchell asks.

I wait until the anger subsides before answering, taking several deep yoga breaths to calm myself. Dad's breathing is mimicking mine, and I know he's doing it to help me stay focused. When I feel more like myself, I nod to him.

"He came here to kill her. He said she didn't deserve the name Graham," I say.

Mitchell slams his palm against the back door. "Damn it! It's Elijah. He probably killed Mindy and then kidnapped Loralei after she married someone else." He eyes me, and even though he doesn't say it, I know he's wondering how Elijah was able to slip through my grasp more than once. That's what I want to know, too.

"We have nothing to book him for," Dad says, being the voice of reason as usual.

"We need to go back to his place and force a confession out of him." Mitchell's hand extends in my direction, pointing at me. "He knows what Piper can do. We can use that to intimidate him."

"If he hasn't cracked yet, he's not going to," I say, leaving off the part where Elijah is good at blocking his thoughts from me if he hid something this huge. We're all already thinking it. "I need to get inside Mindy's house. I'm sure there's plenty in there for me to read."

"I can get a search warrant in motion, but it could take a few days." Mitchell huffs and looks out at the backyard. "I'm willing to bet Mindy is already dead, but Loralei might not be. We need to move."

Sometimes I can sense when someone is dead, but I need a personal belonging to do it, which necessitates getting inside Mindy's house.

"We need to contact Mindy's family. Find out if any of them know she's missing," Dad says.

I nod. "Can you do that while Mitchell and I pay Elijah another visit?" Time is not our friend, and we have too much to do.

"Sure. I'll be at the office. Call me if you need me." Dad puts a reassuring hand on my shoulder and squeezes. He knows it's tough on me when I get a glimpse inside a psycho's mind.

"I'm okay," I tell him.

He smiles at me and then claps Mitchell on the arm. "Take care of my girl."

"She's more than capable of taking care of herself, but I've got her back," he says, knowing I hate to be coddled—especially by him.

We head to our cars, and I wave goodbye to Dad as Mitchell backs out of the driveway.

"How bad was it?" he asks, giving me a sideways glance.

After being inside a criminal mind, I feel unclean like bugs are crawling under my skin. I wrap my arms around myself.

"You don't have to talk about it if you don't want to."

"No, it's fine. He hated her, though. His anger was so intense."

"Well, she did take everything in the divorce. We saw his hatred for her back at his house."

Something feels off. Something I can't quite put my finger on. "It was different in my vision. Heightened."

"Maybe because that was before he killed her. Now that she's dead—most likely—he's probably celebrating inside."

"Celebrating with delivery boxes littering his house?" No. He was upset. Sad. "This doesn't all add up. I'm missing something." Again.

"Maybe he's upset because he thinks we'll catch him and he'll pay with life in prison. You never know how someone will react from taking a human life, even if they hated the person."

He could be right. I've shown Elijah what I can do. He could be worried. He might have handed over the wedding dress because he wanted to appear as though he was cooperating, all the while knowing it could mean getting himself convicted in the end.

By the time we get to Elijah's house, I'm wiped and starving. The hours always get away from me on cases like this. Mitchell and I exit the Explorer in unison and walk up to the front door. He gives me a brief look before knocking. Jezebel barks, so clearly she's back from the groomer, but Elijah doesn't answer the door.

"Elijah, it's Detective Brennan and Ms. Ashwell. We

need to speak with you right away. Please open the door." Mitchell's booming voice probably draws the attention of nearby neighbors. I wouldn't doubt if a few curtains are being pulled aside to see what's going on, but my focus remains on the front door.

Mitchell pounds on the door again, which makes Jezebel bark even louder. I focus on tuning in to the energy inside the house. When Mitchell tries to knock again, I hold up my hand to stop him.

"I don't think he's in there. I can sense the dog but not Elijah."

"Damn it. He probably ran right after we left."

I shake my head. "No. He picked up the dog from the groomer and came back. Then he left. Why would he get the dog if he planned to take off?" Any respectable dog owner would leave the dog in the care of someone if they planned to be gone for a while.

"So do we sit here and wait for him to return?" Mitchell turns around and takes in the neighborhood. "He could be sitting in someone else's house, watching us and laughing his ass off right now."

"There's a pizza place in the strip mall at the front of the development. We could grab a few slices and then park down the road to keep an eye on the place," I suggest.

"Hungry?" he asks.

My stomach answers for me.

"All right. I guess we can grab something and head back here. I hate to leave the house unattended though. I mean, what if Elijah is in there somewhere and the second we leave, he runs?"

I bite my lower lip as I think. "Okay, you go get the pizza, and I'll look around here some more."

"Are you trying to get me to buy you lunch?" Mitchell asks, crossing his arms and cocking his head at me.

"Keep dreaming. It's more like you're totally useless when it comes to getting a read on things, so there's no point in you sticking around here." I shoo him away, which makes him laugh.

"Pepperoni or plain?" he asks when he reaches his Explorer.

"Sausage," I say.

He opens his mouth—I'm sure to make a crude comment—but he stops and gets in the car instead. As soon as he pulls away, I walk around to the backyard. There's a small pen, which I'm assuming is for Jezebel. The rest of the yard is pretty overgrown and in desperate need of some TLC. If this is how he kept the property in Weltunkin when he was married to Mindy, I can see why she left him. I climb the stairs on the back deck and peer in through the sliding glass door. Unlike at Mindy's, I don't get a read on anything. At least nothing pertaining to the case. I continue to look around for several minutes, inspecting the shed out back and even sitting in the worn-out patio furniture. The only read I get off that is of Elijah drunk, watching the stars while Jezebel laid her head in his lap.

My phone vibrates with a text, and I remove it from my purse.

Mitchell: Parked two houses down on the left.

I walk around the other side of the house and nearly step on a shovel lying in the tall grass. Without knowing why, I bend down to pick it up. The energy coming off it stalls my intake of air. I close my eyes and focus on reading it.

Elijah is on his phone, balancing it between his ear and

his shoulder, while banging a shovel against the water valve for the hose. "This damn thing won't budge. It's too rusty." He hits it again. "That bitch gets the house I paid for and leaves me with this piece of crap. All I got in the settlement was this shovel and the other tools in the shed because she wouldn't know what to do with a tool if it hit her on the head." He pauses and turns the shovel over a few times in his hand. "God, I'd love to bash her lying skull right in with this thing." He swings the shovel hard, connecting with the water nozzle.

I drop the shovel and grab my phone.

Piper: Come to the side yard. I found something.

Mitchell doesn't bother to return the text. He just shows up with a concerned look on his face.

I point to the shovel. "Elijah was swinging that at the water nozzle, trying to turn on the hose. He was on the phone and said he wanted to bash Mindy's skull in with the shovel."

Mitchell bends down and examines it. "I don't see any blood, but he'd wash it off if he did follow through with the threat." He carefully picks it up by the handle. "I'll bring it to the station and have it tested for prints and blood. If Mindy put up a fight, her prints could be on it, too."

I don't bother to tell him prints won't be useful. Elijah and Mindy were married. It wouldn't be odd to find both of their prints on something they owned while they lived together. We need to find traces of blood on it.

"What I don't understand is how he was able to fool you when you asked if he hurt Mindy," Mitchell says. "You were reading him at the time, so how did he hide it from you?"

"No one ever has before. I can't explain it."

We walk to the car, and Mitchell puts the shovel in the trunk.

"Are you going to get in trouble for taking that when Elijah wasn't home?" I ask, not that Mitchell has ever been one to play by the rules. He does what he needs to, mostly because it's usually someone's life on the line.

"Don't sweat it. If we find something we can use, I'll deal with it then."

We sit in the car, eating our pizza and watching the house. When it starts to get dark, someone pulls up to the house. A young girl who looks to be college-age. She's tall with long blonde hair. She unlocks the front door and steps inside.

Mitchell and I exchange a glance.

"You think he's dating her?" he asks me.

I open the car door while saying, "Only one way to find out."

We start for the front door when we hear the girl and Jezebel out back. She came to take care of the dog. I walk around the house, and Mitchell follows.

"Hello?" I call to the girl.

She throws the Frisbee to Jezebel and then faces us. "Can I help you?"

Jezebel sees me and rushes right over. I bend down and scratch her on the chin. "Did you miss me?" I ask her.

"Sorry, but Elijah isn't here."

"Who are you?" I ask, continuing to pet Jezebel, who is acting like I'm her favorite person in the whole world.

"I'm Leah. I live across the street in the blue house. I take care of Jezebel when Elijah is away."

Mitchell extends his hand to Leah. "Hi, Leah. I'm Detective Brennan." He dips his head in my direction. "This is Piper Ashwell."

"Is Elijah in trouble?" Leah asks, shaking Mitchell's hand.

"How well do you know him?" I ask, moving toward her in case I need to read her.

"Not very. We're neighbors. When he moved in, he asked me if I could walk his dog for him when he has to be away from home for longer than eight hours. He seems nice enough."

"Do you know where he went?" Mitchell asks.

Leah shakes her head. "I don't ask. I assume it's work-related. He just texts me when he needs me to walk Jez."

"Could we see the text?" Mitchell asks.

Jezebel weaves between my legs, almost knocking me over. I bend down and pet her while Mitchell checks out Elijah's text.

"He doesn't say where he is or when he's returning," Mitchell says, more to me than Leah.

"Like I said, I don't ask and he doesn't tell. He pays me ten bucks each time I come over. It's not much, but it helps put gas in my car. I commute to ESU."

East Stroudsburg University is about twenty minutes from here.

Not wanting to accept that this is yet another dead end, I get a crazy idea. "Leah, would you mind doing something for me?"

"What?" she asks, sounding a little skeptical.

"Since you know Jezebel, would you mind holding her still while I pet her." My gaze flicks to Mitchell, letting him know what I'm up to.

"Why?" Leah asks. "You've been petting her since you got here."

"I know, but she always gets so happy to see me, and

Elijah mentioned she got something in her eye earlier. I'd like to look at it and make sure it's okay."

"Are you a veterinarian?"

"More like a dog whisperer," I say with a smile.

Leah's brows pull together, but she bends down and holds Jezebel by her collar.

The collar. I might be able to read her collar.

"Actually, it's her left eye, so could you stand on her right side?" I ask. "It would make it easier for me to check out her eye." And for me to hold the other side of the collar with my right hand.

Leah seems totally confused, but she gets up, walks around Jezebel, and squats down on her other side. Once she's in position, I take Jezebel's face in my hands and slide my right hand back to grip the collar.

"Good girl," I tell Jezebel as I focus on the collar.

"Well, where is he?"

"Vacation. I'm filling in until he gets back," the woman says, handing the leash to Elijah.

Jezebel wags her tail, happy to see her owner.

"She was a good girl, but I'm told she always is," the woman says.

"Great. Thanks." Elijah walks out of the groomer's and gets Jezebel in the passenger seat of his car.

Once he's in the driver's seat, he turns to Jezebel. "Daddy has to go on a little trip, Jez. Leah will have to take care of you until I get back since Uncle Joel is gone."

"Joel."

"What?" Leah asks.

"Nothing," I say, getting to my feet. "Her eye looks good." I pat Jezebel on the head and turn back to the car.

Mitchell catches up to me in a few steps and gently takes me by my elbow. "What was that about Joel?"

"He's Elijah's brother."

"Joel Underwood? How is that possible? They have different last names."

"Maybe they're half brothers or maybe they're related by marriage. Elijah might have a sister and Joel is her husband. We need to find out if he also works at a dog groomer. Elijah was expecting him to be there when he picked up Jezebel, but the woman who groomed Jezebel said Joel was on vacation."

"Yeah, a vacation in prison for not paying his taxes."

"But then where would Elijah run off to?" I ask.

"Probably wherever he has Loralei."

And we missed our opportunity to follow him.

CHAPTER ELEVEN

By the time I drag my listless body to bed, I'm frustrated and doubting my abilities all together. I thought Joel Underwood was a closed case. One that had nothing to do with Loralei. But now that I know Mindy was attacked, Joel is Elijah's brother, and Elijah is in love with Loralei, I can't make sense of my visions. Do they all fit nicely together? Or is there more than one crime at play here again?

I fall asleep and dream about Jezebel and Loralei burying Mindy's body in someone's backyard. When the phone rings on the nightstand next to me, I jolt upright in a cold sweat.

"Hello?" I answer without bothering to look at the screen to see who is calling or even what time it is.

"Where are you?" Mitchell asks.

"In bed. Why?"

"It's 8:25. I thought we were meeting at eight o'clock."

I pull the phone away from my ear to confirm the time. "I overslept. I'll be there in a few. I just need to jump in the shower."

"I'd make a comment about that, but your dad is right here."

"A comment about what?" Dad's muffled voice asks in the background.

"If you put half as much time into the case as you put into ribbing me, we would have found Loralei and Mindy by now." I toss the covers off, slide my feet into my slippers, and head for the shower. "See you in twenty." I hang up without letting him get in another word, so I'm not all that surprised when the phone rings again before I can even put it down.

"I'll never be ready in twenty minutes if you keep me on the phone."

"Pipe down, Piper." Mitchell laughs. "Hey, that was a good one."

"Hysterical." I roll my eyes even though he can't see me.

"Your dad found out Mindy had planned a vacation at a spa in South Carolina. He called the spa, and they said Mindy never checked in."

"So it's possible this week was planned on purpose because she was supposed to be away."

"Meaning no one would try to check up on her," Mitchell continues for me. "The spa has one of those strict 'no electronics' policies. They don't let you have phones, iPads, laptops, etc. It's all about relaxation and disconnecting."

Perfect when you're trying to murder someone. Mindy is supposed to be off the grid, so no one in her family thought anything was odd when they didn't hear from her. "Did she go by herself?" I ask.

"Yeah. And get this. She booked this months ago before she and Elijah split up. Apparently, it was a wedding present. A couple's getaway."

"So, Elijah was supposed to go. That means he definitely knew she was going, but he didn't say anything about it when we talked to him."

"Of course not. That would make him look extremely guilty."

As if he doesn't already. "Okay, tell Dad I said good work. I'm jumping in the shower now. Then we are going to find Elijah." I hang up and take the quickest shower of my life.

Nineteen minutes later, I open the door to my office. "How's that? A minute early," I say.

"Did you even comb your hair?" Mitchell asks.

I take the elastic hair tie off my wrist and pull my hair into a low ponytail. "Better, Your Highness?" I toss my purse onto my desk and sit down. "Talk to me, Dad. What else do we know?"

"Nothing new since Mitchell called you."

"We're still working on the search warrant for Mindy's place, but if we can find Elijah and get a confession out of him, we won't need to search her house."

"No leads on Elijah, though?" I ask.

They both shake their heads.

"Okay, then what can we do?" I'm not about to sit here and do nothing until someone spots Elijah or our search warrant goes through. I tap my fingernail against the touch pad on my laptop. "What about Loralei's place?"

"What about it?" Mitchell asks, shrugging despite the fact that his hands are in his pockets. "We've already been there."

"True, but now we have more to go on. We know she was involved with Elijah. We know Mindy hated Loralei." My dream comes to mind. "And last night I had a dream Loralei and Jezebel were burying Mindy's body."

Mitchell leans forward, pressing his palms against the desktop. "You think Loralei killed Mindy?"

"I'm not a criminal you're interrogating, Mitchell, so drop the"—I point a finger at him and gesture to his stance —"whatever this is." I rub my forehead, begging these visions to make sense. "Sometimes my visions and dreams are more metaphorical than literal. What if Loralei burying Mindy's body is a metaphor for how Loralei ended Mindy's relationship with Elijah? She buried their marriage six feet under."

"Did you see where she was burying the body?" Mitchell asks. "We might want to check out that location just in case."

I shake my head. "I assume it was Elijah's backyard or Loralei's since both Loralei and Jezebel where there."

"Should we bring Jezebel to Loralei's yard and have her sniff around?"

"Are you proposing we kidnap a dog?" Dad asks. "We have Harry, a trained K9. Some days I think I retired and left you on your own too soon. Maybe you should request a partner."

Mitchell juts his chin in my direction. "I already have one. And now that you've come out of retirement, I have you, too."

And I don't need anyone else from the Weltunkin PD watching me like I'm a freak show. Bringing Mitchell on board has been difficult enough, and he was already familiar with psychic visions.

"Can you call whoever is in charge of Harry and have him meet us at Loralei's place?" I ask Mitchell.

"Yeah. I'll call Wallace." He walks to the other side of the office to make the call, and Dad and I stare at each other.

"I know that look," Dad says. "You're thinking something crazy."

"I was just wondering what the odds were that Steven McNamara set this all up. I mean, he could have found out about Loralei and Elijah and discovered Loralei's plan to run away with him. That could have driven him insane with jealousy, forcing him to resort to kidnapping his own wife."

"I know you don't see everything when you read people, but don't you think you would have seen that?"

I lower my head. "After Elijah managed to keep so much from me, I'm beginning to wonder how much I've missed since this case began."

"Maybe the stress is getting to you. You know that can affect your abilities."

With the way I've been trying to expand my abilities, Dad could be right. I might be putting too much pressure on myself and stifling my abilities in the process. "I think I could use that spa retreat Mindy was supposed to go on."

Dad wheels his chair over and places a hand on my shoulder. "Pumpkin, what you need is to cut yourself some slack. We're still further along in this case than we would be if we didn't have you to give us leads."

"I doubt that. My leads have led us in all the wrong directions."

"Not true. Once we get that search warrant or find Elijah, this case will open right up. I'm sure of it. And you were the one who discovered Joel Underwood is Elijah's brother. We're going to look into him too, which will be easy since he's being detained downtown until the IRS puts him away for a while."

He's right. Joel is the one I need to talk to, even before going to Loralei's. I stand up and snap my fingers to get Mitchell's attention.

His brow furrows. Then he mumbles into the phone before covering it with his hand and saying, "What? I'm not a dog, you know."

"We don't need Harry just yet. I want to talk to Joel first. Set that up for me."

Mitchell looks to Dad as if he can't believe I'm ordering him around.

"You heard her. Chop, chop." Dad snaps his fingers, and he and I laugh as Mitchell shakes his head and returns to his phone call.

———

After a quick brunch courtesy of Marcia—I swear I'd die of hunger if not for her—we head to the station to interrogate Joel Underwood. The second I walk into the small room, Joel's eyes become slits. I guess someone told him I'm the reason he got caught skipping out on his taxes.

"Mr. Underwood, I presume you remember who we are," Mitchell says.

"I heard someone talking about her. About what she can do. I wasn't hurting anybody. Why couldn't you just keep your mouth shut?" Joel looks nothing like he did at Triumph Deliveries. There, he seemed almost pathetic. Here, he's angry. At me.

"Mr. Underwood, we aren't here to talk to you about that. We want to hear about your brother, Elijah."

Joel's face scrunches up. "I don't have a brother."

Mitchell jerks his head in my direction. "He's lying, right?"

I focus on Joel. Reading him without touching him isn't as easy for me as it is for other psychics, but I do my best. "You had a brother at one time, but he's deceased."

"That's why I can't afford to live on my own or pay taxes. My brother had a gambling problem. One that caught up with him."

"Are you saying he was killed because of it?"

"I'm saying he drank himself into a coma. And that left me to pay what he owed." Joel leans back in the hard metal chair, his feet extending out the other side of the small desk.

I stare down at him. "Were you threatened by his bookies?"

"You could say that. I couldn't let my parents find out the truth about A.J. He was the good son in their minds. I'm the screwup." He scoffs. "If they only knew the truth."

"They had to know the true cause of death," Dad says.

"They do. And they think he was a victim of hazing. He died when we were in college."

"So, for the last ten years or so, you've been trying to get back on your feet after paying his debts?" I ask.

Joel nods. "And now, thanks to you, that will never happen."

"Whoa," Mitchell says. "You can't blame Piper for you not paying your taxes. I get being down on your luck and even bailing out your brother, but the entire tax evasion scandal is on your head and your head alone."

"Do you know Elijah Graham?" I ask.

"Never heard of him."

"Did you lie about not knowing Loralei McNamara?" Dad asks.

Joel leans forward in his chair and looks directly at me. "Why don't you tell me? Or are you not really psychic after all?"

Mitchell slams his open palms against the table, making Joel jump. "Listen up. If you are withholding information in a police investigation, you're going to find yourself in more trouble than you ever dreamed."

I place my hand on Mitchell's arm, which is radiating with angry energy, not that I needed my abilities to tell me that. "Let me," I tell him.

Mitchell pushes off the table and puts his back to Joel.

I take the seat opposite Joel and stare at him. Not to read him. Just to make him think I am. "Interesting."

"What is?" Joel asks.

"Care to fill my friends in on what I just saw about your connection to Loralei McNamara?" I plaster a look of contentment on my face to hopefully pull off this ruse.

To his credit, Joel remains quiet and composed.

"No?" I lace my fingers in front of me on the desk. "Okay, but..." I hold one finger in the air and pause for dramatic effect. "You should remember that cooperation can earn you certain favors, while withholding information pertinent to a case will find you in even more trouble. So I'll ask you one more time before I spill your secrets. How do you know Loralei?"

I let Joel fume for a few moments, his nostrils flaring. Then I tap my finger against the desk. "Ticktock, Joel. Time is running out."

"Fine!" he yells. "I looked into the name as soon as you left the warehouse. I delivered a package to her last week. She was fighting with some guy. Really yelling. I could hear it through the door."

"Who was she fighting with? Did you see?" Dad asks.

"Yeah, I saw. He answered the door when I rang the bell. I needed Loralei to sign for the package though, so he brought her to the door. Her eyes were red, like she'd been crying. She scribbled her name, took the package, and I left. End of story."

"What did the man look like?" Dad asks, rephrasing his question.

"I wasn't paying much attention. I do remember he wore glasses, though."

Steven McNamara? "Do you remember what day that was?" I ask.

"You didn't see that, too?" Joel spits out.

"Would you like me to look deeper into your mind? I could, but I figured it would be less intrusive to just ask you. You are choosing to cooperate, aren't you?"

"About that." Joel sits forward again. "I want to make a deal. I can't spend my life in prison. You've got to help me out if I'm going to help you."

I don't have the heart to tell him Mitchell's hands will be tied as far as the IRS is concerned. "We'll do everything we can as long as you continue to help us, Mr. Underwood."

"That's it? I need details, or I'm not talking anymore." He sits back again, crossing his arms in front of his chest.

"I'm assuming they took your personal belongings when you were brought in," I say.

Mitchell smiles and walks to the door. He knocks on the glass, and when the officer on the other side opens the door, they whisper for a moment before it shuts again. "Personal effects are on the way."

"What's that about?" Joel asks. "Are you letting me go?" His eyes widen.

This guy is unbelievably naïve if he thinks for a second that we'd just release him. "No," I say. "I can see what happened for myself if I have a personal belonging of yours. So we're finished here. Good luck with the IRS." I stand up.

"Wait!" Joel reaches for me, latching onto my right hand, which is stupid on his part.

"You can't ask me to do that," Loralei yells.

"We're getting married in two days. Two days, Lor. I can't have my wife conversing with her ex. It's humiliating. You tell me it's over between you two, but I always know when he contacts you. You're different. You still love him."

"I love you," she yells.

"You want to love me. That I believe, which is why I'm asking you to say goodbye to him for good. Once we're married, this has to end."

Joel pulls his hand from mine.

"Thank you, Joel. You've been most helpful," I say.

"What?" His gaze volleys from me to Mitchell to Dad. "What's going on? I'll help you. I'll tell you what I know."

I motion for the door, and Mitchell and Dad follow me out with Joel begging us to stay.

"Well?" Mitchell asks as we walk to his car.

"It was Steven. He knew all about Elijah. Two days before the wedding, he begged Loralei to stop seeing him. Told her it had to end once they were married."

"Then you might be right," Dad says.

"About what?" Mitchell asks. "Why do I feel like I was left out of something?"

"Because you were," I say. "I think Steven set this all up. He gave Loralei an ultimatum. I think she broke it when she met up with Elijah after the wedding."

"And that's why Steven kidnapped her," Mitchell says.

"We need to go talk to the groom."

CHAPTER TWELVE

After telling him what I now know about his fight with Loralei, Steven sobs into his hands on his brown leather couch. Mitchell gives me a look that's nothing short of "Should I cuff him now?" This isn't a confession, though. The waves of energy coming off Steven are making that clear.

"I love my wife," he says between heaving breaths of air.

"I don't doubt you do," I say, "but love can make people do crazy things." I move closer to the couch. "Tell us what really happened the morning after the wedding." I'm more convinced than ever that Steven knows more than he's told us.

He picks his head up, wipes his nose with the back of his hand, and lets out a long, shaky breath that smells of stale beer. I do my best not to cringe because I need him to talk.

"Did you see Loralei after she left this apartment?"

"Yes. I went to her place."

"Why?"

"Because I didn't trust that she'd stay true to her word, and I was right."

"What do you mean you were right?" Mitchell asks.

Steven looks at me. "When she showed up for the wedding, I could tell she'd been crying."

Yeah, because her maid of honor gave her Mindy's garter and reminded her of Elijah, the man she really loved, moments before she had to walk down the aisle.

"Still, she went through with it. We got married. I thought things were okay until we got back here. She said she had a migraine."

"You didn't consummate the marriage?" Mitchell asks, and I'm grateful he at least phrased it respectfully.

Steven shakes his head and sobs. "She said we would on the honeymoon and it would be more special that way. She said she didn't want the memory of our first night together as husband and wife ruined by the pain of her migraine."

I don't need a vision to know that was a lie.

"She got up early and left for her place to pack. I went there to see if she was really home packing or if she was somewhere with him." He pauses to regain his composure, and it takes all my might not to latch onto his arm and see this for myself. I can't just invade his privacy like that when he's hurting. Although, if I get any inkling that he did kill Loralei, I'll do it in a heartbeat.

"Take your time, Mr. McNamara," I say, earning me wide eyes from Mitchell.

"His car was in the parking lot."

"Whose?" Dad says, knowing we need to be absolutely certain of every detail.

"Elijah's." Steven's breathing becomes heavy, his chest rising and falling. "I parked and took the stairs up to her floor. I didn't knock. I couldn't. I think I was too afraid of what I'd find on the other side of that door." He breaks down and cries again, forcing us to wait.

Mitchell tilts his head in Steven's direction, indicating I should just read him. I shake my head. As long as he's talking, I'm not going to cross that boundary.

"He was in there for a while. Twenty-five minutes at least, and who knows how long he was there before I showed up?" He sniffles and wipes his nose on his sleeve. "I stayed in the entrance to the stairwell so no one would see me. I watched him leave. She didn't walk him to the door. Thankfully. I wouldn't have been able to handle it if she'd seen him out and kissed him goodbye."

"What did you do next?" Dad asks, his voice soft and full of compassion. One thing Dad's always been good at is playing the good cop. He can think someone is as guilty as can be and he'll still play nice until he gets the information he wants out of him.

"I watched him leave, and then I knocked on Loralei's door."

"How did she react when she saw you?" Mitchell asks.

"She knew immediately that I had seen Elijah. She said nothing happened. That he begged her not to end things and she sent him away."

So Elijah lied about when he and Loralei had that conversation. It happened *after* the wedding. "Do you believe her?" I ask, purposely phrasing it in the present tense because I need to know how he feels about this now.

"I did at the time. She said she was almost finished packing and she'd meet me at the airport. She kissed me, and I left. That was the last time I saw her."

"And when she didn't show up at the airport, what did you think then?" I ask.

"That she'd played me. That she'd said what she needed

to in order to get me to leave and that she'd run off with him."

Mitchell and Dad both look to me to confirm his story. The problem is I'm not confident in my senses lately. But maybe this is proof I should be. My first impression was that Steven was telling the truth. He loves his wife, and he thinks she left him for Elijah.

"Mr. McNamara, we've spoken with Elijah Graham. He admitted to being in touch with Loralei."

"He's still here? That can't be. I went—" He stops abruptly and lowers his head.

"Were you going to say you went to his house?" Mitchell asks.

"Yes. I had to know if it was true. He wasn't there, though. Not once."

"How many times did you go there?" Mitchell asks.

"Seven," Steven answers without hesitation. "I need to know. I think I deserve to hear it from Loralei."

"We believe Mr. Graham took off," I say. "His neighbor is taking care of his dog."

"Jezebel." Steven scoffs. "Loralei used to tell me she spent the day with Jezebel. I think she thought it wasn't a complete lie if she mentioned the dog by name. Even if it was to mislead me into thinking it was a friend of hers instead of her lover's pet." He covers his face with his hands. "If he's gone, she's with him," he says through his fingers.

"Did she ever mention anywhere she wanted to go?" Dad asks. "Some place she wanted to vacation possibly?"

Steven lifts his head. "Yeah, Aruba. That's why we were going to honeymoon there. I tried to give her everything she wanted, but it didn't matter. She wanted the one thing I couldn't give her. Him. I couldn't be him."

I take a chance and say, "Do you know Elijah's ex-wife is also missing?"

"What? He was married? Was he seeing Loralei at the time? Do you think his ex-wife did something to her?" As hurt as he is, he still wants to make sure Loralei is okay. He's not the kidnapper. I'm sure of it.

"I think someone kidnapped his ex-wife first. She may or may not be alive at this point."

"Are you implying this is a serial killer?" He puts his hand to his chest, which is heaving again. "A serial killer might have my Loralei?"

"Try to calm down, Mr. McNamara. We aren't sure of much just yet," I say.

"Why not? You're psychic. Can't you see where she is? You were at her place, weren't you? Did you search everything?"

No. I searched her things related to the wedding. That's where I went wrong. I need to search her other belongings. The yearbook was a good clue, but I should have gone further from there.

"I have an idea." I stand up. "Mr. McNamara, you've been very helpful. I'll call you as soon as we find out anything. I promise."

"Miss Ashwell," Steven says. "I don't want anything to happen to my wife. Even if she never loves me the way she loves him, she deserves to live a long and happy life."

I nod and walk out of the apartment.

"Was that genuine, or is he the world's best actor?" Mitchell asks when we're in the elevator.

"He was being honest."

"Maybe this time, but he hid this from us. Why?"

"I think he was afraid it would make him look guilty. I mean he caught his new bride with another man."

Mitchell huffs. "I see your point. I definitely would've suspected him."

"We need to find Elijah, and I think searching Loralei's apartment again is the key."

"Want me to call Officer Wallace and get Harry to search her yard?" Mitchell asks, reaching for his phone in his pocket.

"No. I think the dream was metaphorical. What I need is somewhere inside that apartment." I just have no clue what it could be.

————

The apartment complex on Zinnia Court is buzzing when we arrive. Since it's rush hour and everyone is most likely getting home from work, that's not unusual. And it actually works in our favor. I still have the key to Loralei's apartment, and when I open the door, her neighbor pokes her head out into the hallway.

"Can I help you?" she asks us.

Mitchell flashes his badge, making me want to smack him. I could have just told her I'm a friend looking after the plants in the apartment while Loralei is on her honeymoon. But no. Mitchell has to whip out his detective badge to impress the ladies.

"Detective Mitchell Brennan." I've noticed he usually provides his first name when speaking to women. "Do you live in that apartment right there?" He points behind her.

"Yes. Is something wrong? Is Loralei in some sort of trouble?" The woman looks panicked.

"How well do you know Loralei?" I ask.

The woman shrugs. "I've lived here for two years now. Loralei and I run into each other from time to time. She let me take a shower at her place when the landlord was having mine repaired. That's about it. Is she in trouble?" she repeats, lowering her voice since we aren't the only people in the hallway.

"No. I'm Piper Ashwell. I'm a private investigator. This is my father, Thomas Ashwell. We work together. And this is Detective Brennan, as you know. We were working a case nearby, and I promised Loralei I'd water her plants while she was away, so we stopped in."

The woman puts her hand to her chest and sighs. "Phew. I thought maybe something awful happened one apartment over from mine. I watch too many crime shows on TV, and my mind gets carried away with me sometimes."

"When was the last time you saw Loralei?" Dad asks. "You were obviously concerned. Does that mean you haven't run into her in a while?" He's so good at playing it cool. Mitchell should really take notes.

"Oh, um..." She sucks her lower lip into her mouth as she thinks. "I guess it was sometime early last week. Before the wedding. I wasn't invited, but like I said, we're acquaintances not friends."

"Did you see her in passing?" Dad asks. "In the hallway like this?"

"Yeah, I had just gotten home from work and she was on her way out. I assume to meet her fiancé for last-minute wedding stuff."

"Did she say anything to you?" Mitchell asks.

The woman shrugs. "'Hello. How are you?' You know, typical stuff. Why? Are you sure there's nothing going on here?"

Way to make her suspicious again, Mitchell.

"No, Detective Brennan just has trouble conversing normally with people. He's the job, you know." I clamp my hand down on his shoulder. "Always trying to interrogate everyone." I lower my voice and lean toward her. "He has some social issues."

Mitchell's stare pierces the side of my head, but I pretend not to notice.

"Well, I better water those flowers. Loralei will never forgive me if I let her precious plants die."

"That's weird. I don't remember her having any plants, but I was only inside her apartment that one time, so..." She shrugs again and turns back toward her apartment.

"Nice going," I say to Mitchell once we're all inside Loralei's apartment with the door closed.

"What? I was doing my job."

"She didn't need to know that. You saw her. If you told that woman Loralei is missing, she would have had a panic attack, thinking a psycho lived in the building and was kidnapping female tenants. And while I'm sure you would have offered to protect her, we don't have time for you to pick up women while we're on this case."

"I wasn't trying to pick up anyone," Mitchell says.

"Pumpkin, maybe we should start looking around," Dad says, taking me by the arm and leading me to Loralei's bedroom. "You know, for someone who claims not to be attracted to Mitchell, you sure do give him a hard time about women."

"I just don't like witnessing him flirting while we're working. There's a time and a place, and this isn't it."

"Maybe so, but you don't want him to get the wrong impression."

He would, too. Mitchell thinks he's God's gift to women. No doubt he's convinced I'd throw myself at him too if given the opportunity. What an idiot.

"Message received, Dad. I'm ready to fully focus on this case and find Loralei."

"Good." He opens drawers on the dresser and peers inside each one.

I'm not looking for clothing, though. I need something more personal. Something Loralei would have cared about more than a favorite pair of jeans. Maybe even something that was given to her as a gift. Jewelry perhaps. I walk to the tall dresser by the closet and head straight for the jewelry box on top. I lift the lid, hoping to find something she wore often, but instead music fills the bedroom. Familiar music. It's "The Music of the Night" from *The Phantom of the Opera*.

The song fills my head, drowning out everything else and sending chills through my body. Not a single vision comes. Only facts, clear as the air before my eyes. I know why Loralei was taken.

The song ends, leaving me trembling and staring at the figure on the music box that has now stopped dancing.

"Piper?" Dad asks. "What is it?"

"The song. It's why she was kidnapped."

"Someone kidnapped her because of a song?" Mitchell asks in the doorway.

"No. The meaning of the song. That's the answer. It's what I needed to hear." I close the music box and open it again, letting the words linger in the air.

When it finishes, Dad and Mitchell are still staring at me completely confused.

"The words. It's about the Phantom kidnapping Christine because he loved her and she didn't love him back."

"It was a love triangle," Dad says. "Between Christine, Raoul, and the Phantom."

"Just like the love triangle between Loralei, Elijah, and

Steven," Mitchell says. "Is that what you're trying to tell us? Is Steven the Phantom? Did he kidnap her because she loved someone else?"

"No." I know he didn't do it, but someone else did. "The person who kidnapped her also loves her."

"Elijah or someone else all together?" Dad asks.

"I'm not sure. But it fits. Mindy was in Loralei's way so this man, this 'Phantom,' killed Mindy."

"But Mindy was in the way of Loralei and Elijah being together, so then it has to mean Elijah is the killer and the kidnapper." Mitchell stares at me, waiting for me to say he's correct, but I don't know if he is.

"It could be. I mean, he divorced Mindy but she was bleeding his checking account dry, which means he probably couldn't afford to give Loralei the kind of life he wanted to. He'd have to get Mindy out of the way completely first."

"Piper, are these facts, or are you hypothesizing?" Dad asks.

"Hypothesizing based on facts." And now my dream makes sense. "Loralei didn't bury Mindy, but she's the reason Mindy is dead."

"You're certain Mindy isn't alive?" Dad asks.

I nod. "Yes, and I'm certain the killer is the person who gave Loralei this music box. He's reenacting his own version of *The Phantom of the Opera*.

CHAPTER THIRTEEN

"You're certain it's Elijah then?" Dad asks.

I let out a puff of air, ruffling the hair around my face. "Only one way to be sure, right?" I pick up the music box. This time, I don't play the music. I just read the energy off the box.

"You don't know who sent it?" Catherine asks.

"No." Loralei searches the box it was delivered in. "There's no note or anything."

"Do you think it was Steven?"

Loralei opens the music box and sways to the tune. "No. I never told him I love The Phantom of the Opera.*"*

"The song it plays could be a coincidence, though." Catherine reaches for the music box, taking it from Loralei's hands.

"I suppose, but if I ask Steven and he didn't send it..."

Catherine closes the lid. "All hell will break loose. Which begs the question, do you think Elijah sent it?"

Loralei shrugs. "I'll find out." She grabs her phone off the coffee table, but before she can call, Catherine places her hand on top of Loralei's.

"Are you sure? You're weeks away from your wedding. Is talking to Elijah right now a good idea?"

Loralei puts the phone down and presses the heels of her palms against her eyes. "I don't know anymore. I'm not sure of anything. Everyone wants me to marry Steven. Hell, I want to love him. I do. I know Elijah isn't good for me. He never was, but I can't get my heart to accept that."

"Why not marry Elijah and stop fighting this? If things blow up in your face, it could end all of this for good."

"But I'd lose Steven in the process."

"Is that really a bad thing?"

"You were just trying to convince me not to go see Elijah, and now you're saying he's the one I should marry?"

"What can I say? I'm just as confused as you are."

The vision ends. I put the music box back on the dresser. "She doesn't know who sent it because it was delivered directly from the store. I had no sense of who ordered it because he or she must not have ever touched it."

"So it was most likely an online order meant to be anonymous," Dad says.

"If you ask me, that implicates Elijah. He wouldn't put his name on anything Steven might see."

"We need to find Elijah," I say. "And show him this music box so I can see his reaction."

"What about Steven?" Dad asks. "He fits the profile of the Phantom more than Elijah does since in the play, Christine loved Raoul, not the Phantom."

"Right. Elijah is Raoul," Mitchell says.

"I feel like my visions are more muddled than usual," I say. "I'm sorry, guys."

"If you apologize one more time, I'm going to call your mother and have her lecture you like she did when you were a kid." Dad's threat isn't empty by any means. He'd do it in a heartbeat.

"What do we do, Piper?" Mitchell asks, his hands on his hips.

"Mindy is dead. I can feel it in my gut. We can't save her. So we focus on Loralei. Find Elijah, and have an officer keep an eye on Steven. We'll watch his every move to make sure he isn't playing us."

"On it," Mitchell says, whipping out his phone and walking back into the living room.

"You want to keep reading things here?" Dad asks.

"It's been a packed day. I'm wiped out." Tapped out is more like it. The visions are taking a toll on me, and I'm not sure I'm any closer to figuring them out. "Let's call it a night." We can't do anything without knowing where Elijah is anyway. My body needs sustenance and sleep.

Dad wraps his arm around my shoulders, and we meet Mitchell in the living room. He holds up a finger as he finishes his call.

"Keep me posted. No matter what time of day. Thanks." He hangs up and pockets his phone. "Fill me in on the plan."

"Food then sleep," I say.

"Another Ashwell family dinner?" he asks, his voice laced with hope.

Dad looks to me. "I could call your mother."

"No. I want to go home, eat, take a long bath, and fall asleep."

Mitchell's face falls. He doesn't have the kind of family life I do, and I know he loves when we include him in ours. I'm just not up for it.

"Sorry," I say more to him than Dad.

"No problem, pumpkin." Dad leads me out of the apartment.

"I'll be sure to let you both know if the officers staking out Steven's and Elijah's places find either one of them participating in late-night activities," Mitchell says.

I can't help hoping they don't find anything until morning.

———

When I arrive at my office Friday morning, Mitchell is standing at the door with coffees in hand. I take one and immediately slug it.

"Whoa! You're going to burn your mouth and throat," Mitchell says.

"I'm a big girl," I say, putting my key in the lock and opening the door. "Where's my dad?"

"Sleeping in I guess."

"He never sleeps in." I turn on the lights and head for my desk, which looks dwarfed compared to Dad's.

Mitchell laughs. "I love that he bought a desk that's so much bigger than yours."

"I'm starting to think you were a bad influence on him when you two were partners." I toss my purse in the bottom drawer and open my laptop, bringing it out of sleep mode.

"Or maybe you secretly harbor feelings for me because I remind you of your father."

"That's definitely not it," I say, rolling my eyes and taking another sip of coffee. "No word from the officers stationed at Steven's and Elijah's homes?"

"Not a one. I expect Steven will go to work."

"No, he won't. He took a week's vacation because he's

supposed to be on his honeymoon." I type Elijah's name into the search bar of my web browser.

"What are you doing?" Mitchell walks around Dad's desk and sits in his chair, which he wheels over to mine so he can look over my shoulder as I work.

"Are you wearing cologne?" I ask, twitching my nose in his direction.

"It's my aftershave. Do you like it?"

"You smell like a pimp." I pull up Elijah's Facebook profile.

"And you would know what a pimp smells like?" He leans back in his chair. "Tell me, Piper, what else don't I know about you?"

I glare at him quickly before turning my attention back to the screen. Facebook is a dead end. Elijah hasn't posted anything in the last two weeks. I go back to the Google search and scan the results.

"Whoa, scroll back up," Mitchell says.

"To what?"

Mitchell reaches over me and uses the touch pad to find the result he's looking for. "That."

"No way." I click on the link. "Why would he be mentioned in an article about Shady Acres Psychiatric Hospital in Massachusetts?" The headline mentions a patient but not by name.

Residents are displeased by the decision to release long-time patient Joel Wood. Despite the attending doctor's prognosis, many believe that Mr. Wood is not fully recovered and ready to rejoin the public. His past discretions range from petty theft to torturing small animals. Admitted at the young age of nine, Mr. Wood has undergone treatment for mental disorders and depression.

"*Mr. Wood has been the model patient for the past two*

years. If I didn't feel he could be a fully functional member of society, I would not be allowing his release," says Dr. Martinson.

The media has been unable to contact Mr. Wood's family, which only includes his mother, Meredith Graham, and his younger brother, Elijah.

"Oh my God." I press my hand to my mouth. "Elijah does have a brother named Joel." I was right. "But his name isn't Underwood."

"No, it's Wood," Mitchell says. "So your vision was a little off."

No. I know it wasn't. I feel it in my gut. I open a new tab and a new Google search. I type "Joel Wood." It brings up articles on cases brought up against him when he was a child.

"He was a minor, so they threw him in a mental hospital since they couldn't put him behind bars," Mitchell says.

"He was mentally unstable for sure," I say. "There's nothing about him after he was released."

"When was that?" Mitchell asks.

I check the date on the original article I read. "Almost a year ago." Something clicks in my head. "In a vision I saw, Elijah asked the dog groomer where his brother was. He works at Posh Puppy!" I pull up the website and plug the address into my phone's navigation. "He's on vacation. At least that's what the woman told Elijah in my vision. But she can answer some questions for us." I grab my purse and stand.

"Do you think Elijah and Joel are working together?" Mitchell asks.

"I don't know. But I do know I saw Joel's name for a reason. We have to find him."

Mitchell gets us to Posh Puppy in record time thanks to

the flashing light he puts on top of his Explorer. He removes it before we pull in so we don't draw too much attention. I'm out of the car and heading for the entrance the second the car slows to a stop.

"Piper," Mitchell calls, jogging to catch up. "You should let me do the talking."

"Why, because you had the vision and know what the woman Elijah spoke to looks like? Or because you're so good at reading people and objects?" I flash him a look before opening the door and stepping inside.

The place looks like it's trying to cater to rich clients, but if it were, it would be located in Weltunkin, not East Stroudsburg. To the right is the grooming area, closed in with glass walls so people can look right in.

"I can't believe someone caught abusing animals got a job in a pet groomer's," Mitchell says.

"You're right. He'd change his name to cover up who he really is, which means we don't know who to ask for." Elijah never even referred to his brother by his first name in the vision I had of him questioning the woman who works here. "I have an idea," I say. "Follow my lead." I walk over to the glass and tap on it.

The same woman from my vision walks over to us with a miniature poodle in tow. "Can I help you?" Her eyes go right to Mitchell. No surprise there.

"Yes, actually I'm taking care of Elijah Graham's dog, Jezebel, while he's away this week, and she had an unfortunate encounter with a skunk. I was wondering if maybe Elijah's brother was around to make a house call and help me out. I have her in the garage right now, but it's been getting cold at night, and I don't want to keep her there for too long."

Mitchell smiles at me, happy with the story I've concocted.

"Mr. Underhill has the week off."

Underhill. Wood. Underwood. I saw Joel Underwood because my abilities were trying to get me to connect Joel Wood and Joel Underhill!

"Oh no." I feign disappointment. "You don't happen to know where he went, do you?"

"Or maybe have his number so we can get in touch with him?" Mitchell says. "Elijah is at one of those spa retreats that don't allow phones or technology of any sort. We have no way to reach him."

"I can't give out an employee's personal information. I'm sorry," the woman says.

"We understand." Mitchell moves closer to her, a smile on his face. "We wouldn't want to get you in any sort of trouble with Mr. Underhill or your boss. Unless, of course, you are the boss. You look like you could easily handle running this place."

He's laying it on so thick my stomach churns. I should have eaten something with my coffee.

"I'd be happy to tell Mr. Underhill that Elijah left his number as an emergency contact. I wouldn't have to mention your name or this conversation at all." Mitchell is standing as close as possible without actually touching the woman, and her eyes are locked on his.

"Well, I suppose you can't let the poor dog suffer."

We could put the dog in the car and drive her here if the story were the least bit true, but this woman seems intent on pleasing Mitchell. "One moment." She turns and walks through a door in the back, bringing the poodle with her.

"How was that?" Mitchell asks.

"Sickening."

"It worked, didn't it? And I didn't even need to pull out my badge."

No, that's tucked under his shirt. "I'm surprised you didn't pull out something else," I say, and Mitchell doesn't have time for a retort because the woman is walking back over to us with a card in her hand.

She holds it out to him, but then snatches her hand back. "You promise you won't tell Joel I gave this to you?" Her tone is flirtatious, and I have to restrain myself from rolling my eyes.

"Cross my heart," Mitchell says, drawing an X over his chest.

"We really appreciate your help, um..." I pause, waiting for her to supply her name.

"Cheryl." She hands the card to Mitchell. "I put my name and number on here for you, too. You know, just in case." She winks at him.

I grab his arm and shove him toward the door, calling "Thank you" over my shoulder at Cheryl. "I swear, you're like a horny teenage boy."

"What? I got us Joel's number." He holds up the card and flicks it with his free hand. "Who cares how I got it?"

"Let's go back to my office. My dad should be there by now, and I need a scone before the coffee churning in my stomach comes hurling back up thanks to your little show in there." I jerk a thumb over my shoulder as I get in the Explorer.

I call Dad's phone on the way, mostly to avoid having to talk to Mitchell, but it goes straight to voice mail. "That's weird." I dial my office phone next, thinking Dad just forgot to turn on his cell this morning. But that rings four times before the voice mail picks up.

"Try his house," Mitchell suggests.

I do, and Mom picks up on the third ring.

"Hello?" A loud humming in the background practically drowns out her voice.

"Mom. What's that noise?" I ask.

The other end of the line goes silent. "Sorry. I was vacuuming. What's going on, sweetie? Is your father getting on your nerves? I told him to return that desk and get the smaller version. He just won't listen."

"No, I'm actually calling because Dad isn't answering his phone or the office phone. I thought maybe he was still at home."

"What do you mean still? He left the house at seven and said he was going to the office."

I don't want to send Mom into a panic, but my intuition is buzzing. "Oh, that's right. He said he was going to head to the station first. I totally forgot. Sorry about that, Mom."

"No problem, sweetie. Have a good day. Go get those bad guys."

"Thanks, Mom. I will." I hang up and stare at the glove compartment.

"What's wrong?" Mitchell asks.

"He left the house at seven and was headed for the office." I swallow the lump in my throat.

"I know that look. What are you sensing, Piper?"

"Something's happened to my dad."

CHAPTER FOURTEEN

Mitchell grabs the light and puts it on top of the car so we can get back to my office quicker. Then he uses the Bluetooth to call the station and make sure Dad didn't really go there to follow up on a lead without telling us, not that he would. He would have texted me at the very least.

"Sorry, but he hasn't been here," Officer Wallace says.

"Okay, thanks. Oh, and Wallace, I need you to run Joel Underhill through the system and let me know what turns up. I'm looking for an address or anything else you can get me."

"I'm on it."

Mitchell disconnects the call. "Don't let your mind go to that place, Piper. We don't know anything for sure yet."

That's the problem. I don't know, and I should. He's my dad. If he's in trouble, I should have sensed it.

"Can you read something of his at the office and find out what happened?"

"That's the plan," I say. The second step of my plan involves castrating whoever took my father.

Mitchell pulls up to my office, and I race inside. I immediately sit down in Dad's desk chair. He hasn't had this desk long, so there isn't much energy to read off of it. I search the drawers. Nothing but pens, some Post-it notes, and a stapler. I slam the drawer shut.

"Deep breaths, Piper." Mitchell mimics the breathing, like he's seen my father do to get me to focus.

I'm about to tell him he wouldn't be so calm if it were his father who might have been kidnapped by a psycho, but before the words leave my mouth, I remember he doesn't talk to his father. His father won't even look at him or his brother because they remind him of his dead wife.

I ignore Mitchell and look around for anything I might be able to read.

"Hey, what about this?" Mitchell asks, bending down to pick something up off the floor. When he stands, he hands me a ring.

"That's Dad's ring from the police force. They gave it to him when he retired." I hold it in my hand. "There's no way this would have fallen off his finger, so why is it here?"

Mitchell motions to the ring. "Find out."

I take a deep breath, afraid of what I'm going to see. I focus on the ring as I close my eyes.

"Detective Thomas Ashwell?"

Dad looks up from his laptop. "Yes, that's me."

The man standing in the doorway has dark hair and brown eyes. "I'm so glad I caught you."

"How do you know me? I just started working here with my daughter. She hasn't even put my name on the sign yet," Dad says, motioning to the sign in the window.

"Yes, I'm aware. I'm also aware of your daughter's abilities. You must be so proud." He moves toward Dad, who is suddenly looking more alert.

"How can I help you?" Dad asks, playing along.

"You see I'm having woman troubles."

"I don't think you're in the right place then."

The man laughs. "Oh, but I am. You see it's your daughter who is causing the trouble."

"You know Piper?"

"No, which is what makes it all the more bothersome. I don't know her. She doesn't know me. Yet she keeps sticking her nose in my business."

"Who are you exactly?" Dad asks, remaining seated for some strange reason even though he's clearly put off by this strange man.

"You mean you don't know?" The man smirks. "No, I guess you wouldn't. But if Piper were here, she would. Which is why I need you to come with me."

"I'm not going anywhere with you, Mr...."

He laughs. "Nice try, but I didn't get to this point by being dense. Stand up, Mr. Ashwell." The man removes a gun from the inside of his jacket and aims it at Dad.

Dad raises his hands in the air. His ring, visible moments earlier, now nowhere to be seen. "No need for violence."

"That's yet to be determined."

The vision fades, and I'm gripping the ring so tightly it's formed a circle on my palm.

"I think I know what Joel Underhill looks like," I say. "He took my dad."

"But why? How would he even know about your father?"

I think back, trying to figure out where I've messed up. "Elijah could have told him."

"Okay, that's true, but why would he take your father? That's like putting a giant target on his head. We didn't even know who he was until this morning."

"He must have felt we were getting too close to figuring it out." It's the only plausible explanation.

"Maybe. Or..." Mitchell wags a finger in the air. "*The Phantom of the Opera* thing. He spied on Christine, right?"

I nod.

"What if Joel was spying on Loralei?"

"I don't see where you're going with this." I'm too busy thinking of all the horrible things Joel might be doing to my father right now.

"He could have bugged her apartment. And if he did, then he would have heard everything we said when we were there. Both times."

My intuition is humming. "That's it. He bugged her place. He knows all about us. That's how he's evaded us, but when I made the connection to *The Phantom of the Opera*, he got scared he was going to be discovered. So he struck first by taking my dad."

"Do you think he's going to use your dad to buy his own freedom?" Mitchell asks.

"That or this is one big diversion tactic. He knows I'll go searching for my father, which stops me from searching for him and Loralei, allowing him to leave the country with her if he wants to." I lean forward on Dad's desk, resting my head in my hands. "He's going to win."

"Are you sensing that, or is it fear talking?" Mitchell sits down on the edge of the desk.

"I can't lose my dad. He's supposed to be retired. He shouldn't be in harm's way anymore, but I asked him to work with me."

"Stop it." Mitchell stands up and gives me a stern look. "Your father chose to work with you. He bought that insane desk and everything. You didn't do this. So get up, and help me find him before something bad does happen to him."

"Are you scolding me?"

Mitchell crosses his arms, trying to look tough. "I'm just doing what I think your father would do in this situation. He's the best partner I've ever had aside from you."

"He's the only partner you've ever had aside from me." I sniffle and wipe my damp cheeks.

"Which makes him my favorite," Mitchell says with a smirk. "Come on. Wallace is looking for anything on Underhill. We'll find him. In the meantime, we need you to find your dad. If the ring didn't work for giving you the right vision, what will?"

"The more personal the effect, the stronger my visions," I say, standing up and knowing exactly what I need to do. "Dad has his wedding ring on him, so I need something else."

Mitchell's eyes widen when he realizes where I'm going with this. "We have to go tell your mom, don't we?"

"I can't search his room without her knowing." This is going to kill her. In all his years on the police force, he's been injured but never kidnapped. One case as a private detective with me and he gets kidnapped by a certified psychopath.

"I'll drive," Mitchell says.

———

Mom opens the door and smiles at us. "Piper, why didn't you use your key?"

Because I'm not thinking clearly at all. "I left my keys at home," I lie.

"Oh, well come on in. I just made a fresh batch of chocolate chip cookies. Your father was craving them this morning, so I thought I'd surprise him." She looks around Mitchell. "Where is Thomas?"

I step inside, and Mitchell follows. "He's not here," I say. "Come on. Let's go sit down in the living room."

Mom's not having it, though. She holds up her hand to stop me. "Piper Rose Ashwell, you aren't going anywhere until you tell me where your father is."

"That's going to be a problem considering I don't know."

Mom's eyes widen. "He wasn't at the office?"

"Can we please sit down so I can fill you in on the situation?" I motion toward the living room.

She looks shell-shocked, but she allows me to walk her into the living room, where we sit down on the couch. Mitchell remains standing at my side.

I slowly, and as gently as possible, fill her in on what happened. When I'm finished, she raises her hand to her mouth.

"This is all my fault. I couldn't handle having him here all the time, getting in my way and always asking me what I was doing, so I sent him to work with you. I was so selfish. If I'd only..." Sobs cut off her words.

"It's not your fault, Mom. You never could have known this would happen." I wrap my arms around her.

Mitchell leans down toward me and whispers, "I see where you get it from. The Ashwells like to blame themselves."

I ignore him and rub Mom's back. "I need to read something of Dad's. The ring he left in the office is too new to read much from it."

Mom's head bobs. She knows how this works. "What can I do?" she asks, looking completely helpless. If I tell her nothing, it will just send her into another fit of sobs.

"Can you bring me something of his that he wears often? If it's metal, that's even better." I could easily get it myself, but she needs something to occupy her.

She nods again and stands up.

Mitchell starts to go after her, but I reach for him and say, "Let her go. She needs a moment to compose herself."

Mitchell's phone rings, and when he answers, he holds it between us so I can hear as well. I'm assuming he doesn't put it on speaker in case the news he's about to get involves Dad. Mom can't handle overhearing that right now, unless it's to say someone found him alive and well. My intuition is telling me this isn't good news, though.

"Brennan," Mitchell answers.

"It's Wallace. I looked up Underhill. All that came up was a PO Box and a record of employment at Posh Puppy. No physical address in the system, which means he probably lives with someone and just pays rent. I can't even find a bank account anywhere. And that phone number you gave me is no longer in service."

"Okay, thanks for checking into him. I need another favor now." Mitchell's gaze flicks to mine. "Thomas Ashwell is missing. Piper believes Underhill took him because she was getting too close to pinning Loralei McNamara's disappearance on him as well as Mindy Graham's murder."

"Did you say murder?" Officer Wallace asks. Not all of the officers at Weltunkin PD believe in my abilities. At least not my psychic abilities. They think I'm nothing more than a successful private investigator, doing things the old-fashioned way.

"She's dead," I say into the phone.

"How did you find out?" Wallace asks.

"Same way as always. I saw it. Underhill is performing a

dangerous reenactment of *The Phantom of the Opera*. Loralei is his Christine."

"Never saw it. You know where Mindy Graham's body is?" he asks, skepticism filling his voice.

"No," I say through gritted teeth. "I'd find it for you, but I'm a little busy trying to prevent my father from suffering the same fate."

"Right." Wallace clears his throat. He's always liked my dad. "Any leads on where he might be?"

"I'm working on it. In the meantime, I'm assuming your search turned up a picture of Joel Underhill."

"No. There's virtually nothing on him. He doesn't exist on social media or anywhere else."

"That's okay. Piper can send you a sketch," Mitchell says.

He was really impressed with my last drawing from a vision, so I'm not surprised when he suggests it.

"You do that. I'll get as many men as possible out there looking for him."

"Thanks, Wallace. We'll be in touch." Mitchell hangs up just as Mom comes back into the living room.

"I found his watch." She gives a small laugh. "He wore it every day when he was on the force, but he hasn't worn it much since he retired. He called it his good luck charm because we gave it to him on his birthday. Do you remember, Piper?"

"I remember," I say, clasping my left hand over the watch she's holding.

She nods and tries to give me a brave smile. "You'll find him. I know you will."

As much as she's trying to be encouraging, the pressure behind the words nearly suffocates me. I take the watch and stare at it for a moment.

"Here," Mitchell says, removing the pad and pen from inside his jacket. "The sooner we get that sketch to Wallace, the sooner we'll have help finding Underhill and your dad."

I take the pad and pen and walk over to the couch. I don't want to collapse during the vision, and my emotional investment in this could cause me to do just that. I take a few deep breaths, willing myself to be strong for Dad's sake.

Mitchell sits next to me. "I'm right here. No matter what you see, we'll bring him home."

He means dead or alive. I don't want to bring my dad home to bury him.

"Piper," Mom says, reaching for my hand. "Every day of your father's life, since the first time you had a vision, he's been filled with fear. Fear of something happening to you because of what you can do. He's had to push that aside to allow you to grow up and become the woman you are now. You are your father's daughter. If he could find that strength day in and day out, you can now."

I swallow hard and nod. I close my eyes and picture dad in my mind before transferring the watch from my left hand to the right. The energy pulses from the watch, and I try to hone in on Dad right now. In this moment.

It's dark and cold.

I can't see more than a few feet in front of me. No. Not in front of me. In front of Dad. He reaches forward, fumbling with something cold and metallic. A lock on a cage. He's inside a cage. A dog crate.

I listen for sounds, but other than Dad's grunts as he tugs on the lock, there's nothing.

He grips the sides of the crate and starts rocking the whole thing back in forth. It bangs against the ground.

A dog barks. Not just any dog. Jezebel.

I open my eyes. "I know where he is."

Mom covers her mouth with her hand and sobs. "Is he...?"

"He's alive," I reassure her before turning to Mitchell. "We have to go now."

"Where?" Mitchell asks.

"Elijah's. I think Dad's in the basement." I leave off the part about the dog crate because I'm not sure Mom can handle that right now. I start for the door, but Mitchell grabs my arm.

"Piper, that's impossible. We have an officer watching Elijah's place. His reports have shown only Leah has gone in and out of the house to walk the dog."

"But I heard Jezebel."

"You're sure it was her? How can you tell one bark from another?"

"It has to be her." My eyes land on Mom. She's clutching her hands together in front of her, trying not to break down completely.

"Mom, where's Max?" I ask.

"Out back. I need to let him in."

My parents have a fenced in yard because Max loves being outdoors.

"You go get him. I'll call you as soon as I know anything." I kiss her cheek, and Mitchell and I head for his car.

"Max was barking. Maybe the sound infiltrated your vision somehow."

I get in the Explorer and ponder his words. Once he's inside, I say, "I want to check Elijah's place myself."

"We'd need a search warrant. I can get it in motion, but you know the deal. It could take days."

I don't have days. I don't have minutes. I want my dad

back now. "I should go on my own. Then you won't be responsible for any laws I break."

"Absolutely not." Mitchell presses his foot down on the gas pedal, propelling the Explorer forward. "I have an idea."

CHAPTER FIFTEEN

Officer Andrews is sitting in his patrol car sipping a giant cup of soda and has a wrapped burger from Wendy's in his other hand when we pull up to Elijah's house. It reminds me that I only eat on the go these days, and I don't even remember if I ate today. He lowers the window when he recognizes us.

"What are you two doing here?" he asks with his mouth full of burger, which I now see has bacon on it. My stomach rumbles.

"Piper suspects her father might be in the basement. Have you seen anything?"

"Detective Ashwell?" Officer Andrews puts the cup and burger down and gets out of the car.

Mitchell and I get out as well.

"I believe the kidnapper we're looking for in the McNamara case is Joel Underhill, formerly Joel Wood. Have you ever heard of him?" I ask.

"No. Should I have?"

"Probably not. He's been in a psychiatric hospital for most of his life," Mitchell says.

"And now you think he has Detective Ashwell?" Officer Andrews's tone makes it clear that respect for my father is great in the Weltunkin PD.

"Has anyone been watching the back of the house?" I ask.

Officer Andrews shakes his head. "We've been watching for Elijah Graham. We had no reason to think he'd try to slip in through the back. He doesn't even know we're looking for him."

"We need to check it out," I say.

"You can't just go inside," Officer Andrews says, his gaze going to Mitchell for support on this.

"I didn't say I was going to. I'm going to see if I can get a glimpse inside the basement."

"And if not, we're going to ask the dog walker to let us in," Mitchell says. His plan is to con Leah into getting us inside. It's something I'd come up with. Even though she doesn't have the right to invite us in, it doesn't change the fact that it's not breaking and entering. Perfectly legal.

"You sure about this?" Officer Andrews asks Mitchell.

Mitchell ignores him and turns to me, saying, "Shall we?"

"Let's go."

"Keep watch for Elijah," Mitchell yells over his shoulder at Officer Andrews.

"Think he'll rat us out?" I ask as we walk around to the back of the house.

"For what? We aren't breaking any laws."

"Peering in windows?" I challenge.

"Look, if there's someone being held hostage, rules don't apply. We protect the public, and Thomas Ashwell is one of our own, so that makes him a top priority."

I'm glad to hear him say that.

We walk up to the basement door. It's solid, and a jiggle of the doorknob confirms it's locked. I knew it wouldn't be that easy. A small window sits high up on the foundation.

"Can you give me a boost?" I ask Mitchell.

He nods as he walks over to position himself under the window. He gets down on one knee. "Now don't get too excited. I'm not about to propose."

"This is not the time for one of your bad jokes," I say, propping one foot up on his bent knee without bothering to wipe the dirt off my shoe first. I press my hands against the cement foundation as I step up, balancing on one foot.

The basement is dark, which fits my vision. It also means I can't see a thing. I decide to bang on the window, hoping it will illicit some sort of audible response.

Jezebel barks from somewhere inside the house.

"That's the same bark. I'm sure of it," I say. "My dad is in there." I hop down off Mitchell's leg. "We need to go get Leah right now."

As we cross the street to the blue house Leah pointed out to us, Mitchell gives Officer Andrews a nod.

"You love that he can't bust you for this, don't you?" I ask.

"Just like you love that he's going to look like a moron when we walk your father out of there."

I'm going to have a ridiculously big grin on my face when I bring Dad out of that house alive. But not because I'll be showing Officer Andrews I was right. It will be because I got to my dad in time.

Mitchell knocks on Leah's door since there's no doorbell. No one answers at first, and Mitchell is about to knock again when the door swings open. Leah rubs her eyes like she just woke up.

"Sorry, I was taking a nap on the couch. You're lucky it's

Friday. I only have one class, and it's first thing in the morning. If you'd come yesterday, I would have been out most of the day. My schedule is packed on Thursdays." She's even chatty when she first wakes up.

One class and it's first thing in the morning. That's how Joel got my dad into the house without running into Leah.

"Leah, do you remember us?" I ask.

"Of course, but I'm not sure why you're here."

"We need you to let us inside Mr. Graham's house," Mitchell says, producing his badge from under his shirt.

"I'm afraid I can't do that."

"Leah, I know you're probably afraid of getting in trouble, but we need to get inside that house. It's a matter of—"

She holds up her hand. "No, I mean I literally can't let you inside the house. I don't have a key anymore."

"What? Why not?" I ask. There's no way Elijah came home. Not unless Officer Andrews is the worst cop ever.

"Mr. Graham's brother stopped by last night to get the key. I guess he was away and that's why he couldn't watch Jezebel for Elijah. He's back now, though, and I'm officially off doggie duty."

"His brother?" Mitchell asks. "Did he give you his name?"

"Yeah. Joel something. He has a different last name than Elijah. Why? Is something wrong with Jez?"

"No," I say. "Thank you for your help. Sorry to have interrupted your nap." I turn and walk back down the porch steps. I march straight over to Officer Andrews's car and rap my knuckles on his window.

He jumps and then lowers the window.

"He walked right past you."

"Who?" Officer Andrews lifts his gaze, and I'm sure Mitchell is behind me.

"Joel Underhill was next door at the dog walker's house," Mitchell says.

"He walked right past you, and you did nothing!" I scream.

Officer Andrews tosses his burger aside again. "Of course he did. We had no idea we were looking for Joel Underhill. We don't even know what he looks like."

No, because I didn't give them a sketch yet. I was so caught up in my vision of Dad in that dog crate I forgot to sketch Joel.

"Look, Miss Ashwell, your father is a great man and I have the utmost respect for him, but you aren't a member of the Weltunkin Police Department. You can't go ordering us around just because you have a *feeling* about something."

That's it. People who oppose what I do this vehemently usually do it because they have something to hide. I reach forward and grab his shoulder.

"Where were you?" the blonde woman asks, throwing the dish towel on top of the stove and glaring at Officer Andrews.

"Working. Where else?"

"Really? And what case took you to the strip club?"

Officer Andrews's entire body stiffens.

"Mary saw you. She was driving by the place and saw you walking out with some stripper on your arm. How could you, Kurt? You know how I feel about those places. Going is bad enough, but to walk out with one of the strippers?"

"I was only walking her to her car. One of her customers has been giving her a hard time. She's scared."

"So she called the cops? Is that it?"

"Yes! That's exactly what happened. What did you expect me to do? I had to go check it out."

"Were you assigned to this case, or did you volunteer so you could have a little fun under the pretense of working?"

"I was available, so I volunteered. There's nothing else to read into it." He removes his jacket and tosses it over the chair at the kitchen table. *"Now can I have my dinner? It's been a long day."*

"You told me you wouldn't go back there. You said you were through with that life."

"I haven't been back there," he fumes as he sits down at the table. His left hand clenches and unclenches.

"Get her off me!" Officer Andrews yells. "Or so help me, I'll put this window up, and I don't care if it severs her arm in the process."

Mitchell pulls me back, and I glare at Andrews.

"You lied to your wife."

"What?"

"You have a problem. You're a married man who likes to watch women strip."

Mitchell's head jerks in my direction. "That's what you saw?"

I nod. "You disgust me, Officer Andrews. I hope your wife leaves you, because she should." I walk off toward Elijah's house.

A car door slams behind me, and Officer Andrews yells, "I can't let you break in there."

"We have reason to believe Detective Ashwell's life is in danger if we don't get inside that house," Mitchell says. "Probable cause gives us every right to break in."

I don't even bother to turn around. I don't stop until I'm at the basement door.

"Let me." Mitchell holds up a crow bar. "I took this from my trunk while you were storming off. For a second I debated waiting to see how you intended to get inside, but I figured I'd better come prepared."

"No need. I wasn't operating under the delusional

assumption that you were man enough to kick the door in. I came prepared." I reach inside my purse and grab my lock-pick kit.

"You carry a lockpick kit?" Mitchell asks.

"Don't you?" I shrug and continue working on the lock.

He smirks at my comment. Once I get the door open, Mitchell removes his gun from the holster and motions for me to stay behind him. He reaches his free hand along the wall, looking for a light switch. When he finds it, the soft hum of fluorescent lights fills the basement. And then the room begins to come into view.

It's completely empty save for the dog crate in the far corner.

"Dad!" I rush past Mitchell to my father.

"Piper, I knew you'd find me if I left my ring."

"I wish it were that easy," I say, immediately getting to work on the combination lock.

"Where is Joel?" Mitchell asks Dad.

"I don't know. He dumped me here."

Jezebel must hear us because she starts barking upstairs. "He left the dog, too," I say. "We'll have to take her. She'll die on her own here with no one to feed her."

"Did Joel say anything to you?" Mitchell asks Dad.

"He just let me know what a big fan he is of Piper's."

"Sure he did." I pop the lock open and slide it off the crate. Then I flip the latch and open the door.

Dad is slow to get out. I'm sure his back, not to mention everything else, is cramped from being inside there all day.

"Come on. Let's get you home," I say, wrapping an arm around him.

"Piper," Mitchell says. "Stop and think. We're inside Elijah's home. We had a reason to break in, but we aren't going to get another opportunity without a search warrant.

So why don't we take our time getting the dog and try reading a few of Elijah's belongings?"

He's right. Finding Dad was just one of the cases we have to solve. I still need to find Loralei and Mindy's body.

"Dad, do you know if Elijah is helping Joel?" I ask him as we head for the stairs.

"I didn't see Elijah. Only Joel. But why would Joel bring me here? That I couldn't figure out. If Elijah is helping him, why would he implicate himself further by leaving me here?"

"That doesn't add up," Mitchell says. "So maybe Elijah took off because he realized his brother was behind all this."

"You think he's trying to stop Joel?" I ask.

Mitchell just shrugs.

The second we get upstairs, Jezebel greets me with kisses. I bend down and pet her head. "Hi, sweet girl. I'm so glad you're okay."

"I'll grab some food and bowls for her," Mitchell says.

Dad is stretching his neck back and forth. "I'll take a look around. See if I can find anything that will tell us where Joel is hiding."

"He can't be far considering he was able to kidnap you and leave you here after hearing us in Loralei's apartment."

"You think he had the place bugged?"

"Mitchell actually figured that one out," I tell him.

"Don't sound so surprised, Piper. Mitchell is great at his job."

"His laptop is password protected," Mitchell says, coming back into the room, carrying a bag of dog food and two bowls.

"So we don't know if Elijah and Joel kept in touch or not. Joel could be trying to punish Elijah by eliminating the women he cares about." As soon as I say it, it feels off.

That's not it. I rub my forehead. Being in Elijah's place with his things is helping me tap into his energy without even touching his belongings. I guess that's because the house is technically his belonging, even though he hasn't lived here for long.

Still, I walk over to the coffee table and place my hand on top of his laptop.

"You bastard! No matter what I do I can't get rid of you. I swear if you hurt her in any way..."

It's short but tells me what I need to know.

Elijah and Joel don't have a good relationship. They never did. "Elijah didn't want his brother to be released from the psychiatric hospital. He doesn't want him in his life at all. I think he only took Jezebel to Posh Puppy to keep an eye on Joel because he was afraid of what his brother is capable of."

"So Joel is trying to punish Elijah," Mitchell says.

"No. That doesn't feel right. It's more than that. He wants something else, but I don't know what it is." I can't get enough of a read on Joel because he was only ever here to stash Dad.

"So where is Elijah?" Dad asks.

"With Joel," I say, the words just coming off my lips as fact.

"Then are they working together or not?" Mitchell asks. "I can't keep up here."

"They're not. I think Elijah went after Joel to try to stop him."

"Pumpkin," Dad says, placing his hand on my shoulder. "Are you saying Joel has Elijah, too?"

"Yes." The number of people I have to try to save keeps going up.

CHAPTER SIXTEEN

Mom throws her arms around Dad the second she opens the door. Their reunion brings tears streaming down my cheeks, and even Mitchell looks a little misty-eyed. I don't want to intrude on their moment, so I say, "We're going to go. Dad, I'll call you in the morning, but for now you should take some time off to recuperate."

Mom mouths, "Thank you," over Dad's shoulder and pulls him inside before he can protest.

Mitchell drops me off at my apartment, but as I get out of the car, I say, "You want to come inside for a while? We could order some food and talk this case through."

He cuts the engine and undoes his seat belt. "If you want me to have dinner with you, you could just say so." He smiles to show he's only teasing.

I open the back door and let Jezebel out, and Mitchell carries her food and bowls for me.

As luck would have it, we run into my landlord on the way inside.

"Hello, Mr. Hall," I say, trying to sound casual even

though I know we aren't allowed to have pets in the building.

"Ms. Ashwell, I hope you aren't bringing that dog inside."

"For the sake of honesty, I am. You see, she's part of a case I'm working on with Detective Brennan and my father. By the way, Dad said to tell you he says hello."

"How is Thomas doing?" Mr. Hall asks.

"He's had a rough day. This case actually got him kidnapped today, but he's home and recovering. That's why I have Jezebel here. I couldn't leave her with Mom and Dad while Dad is recovering."

Mr. Hall eyes Mitchell. "What about him? Couldn't he take the dog? Or a shelter?"

"Jezebel is a good dog, Mr. Hall. She's really no trouble at all, and she's fully house broken. I can assure you no damage will come to the apartment at her hand."

"Paw," Mitchell says.

I glare at him, wishing he'd shut up and stop trying to help.

"I'd really appreciate it if you could make an exception just this once. And if anything should happen to the apartment because of Jezebel, I'll personally pay to fix it."

Mr. Hall sighs. "Your dad's okay?"

"He'll be fine."

"Tell him I'll give him a call in a few days after he's had time to recover from his ordeal. And the dog can stay *temporarily*." He stresses the last word.

"Thank you, Mr. Hall. Really. You're a lifesaver." I hurry inside before he has time to change his mind.

"Nice work out there," Mitchell says, pressing the button for the elevator.

"Luckily, Jezebel is a good girl. Aren't you?" I bend

down and scratch her chin, earning me a big, wet lick straight up the center of my face.

"Why do dogs like you so much?" Mitchell asks.

"Simple. I can read them. They sense that I can understand what they want, and that makes them more comfortable around me."

"Interesting that your abilities make dogs comfortable and humans *un*comfortable."

The elevator arrives, and we step inside. I press the button for the third floor. "Are you saying I make you uncomfortable?"

"You have. Not so much anymore, but it's been a while since you've read me against my will."

"That could change." I hold my hand out toward him, but he doesn't even flinch, which takes all the fun out of my empty threat.

Mitchell whips out his phone and orders Chinese food from the place just down the block. "I swear all I eat is food from cartons anymore. Except for when I get invited to Ashwell family dinner night."

"That's days away, and no one said you were invited next week." I step off the elevator and head for my apartment, key in one hand and Jezebel's leash in the other.

"We'll see about that," Mitchell says.

The second I open the door, Jezebel runs right inside like she owns the place. She stops in front of the couch, and I know she's thinking of jumping up on it.

"Down," I say, hoping she knows that word.

She sits and lets out a little whimper.

"My money is on the dog," Mitchell says with a smirk, putting the bag of dog food on the floor in the kitchen. He fills up one bowl with water and the other with some food.

"You're probably right considering I couldn't train you to act like a guest here instead of making yourself at home."

"You love it. Tea with dinner?"

I nod. "I haven't eaten all day. Again. This is getting insane." I rub my empty belly.

"And you really can't afford to lose any weight, which is why I ordered plenty of extra."

My weight has always been an issue. "I happen to have a fast metabolism. I'm not this skinny from lack of eating." At least that wasn't the case before Steven McNamara came into my life. "Usually."

Jezebel runs over and sits down next to her food bowl.

"Why isn't she eating?" Mitchell asks.

I pet Jezebel's head. "Because she's a good girl and is waiting to be told she can." I lower my voice. "Try teaching that one to do that." I nod in Mitchell's direction.

"Go ahead," Mitchell says, but Jezebel doesn't budge.

"Eat, Jezebel," I say, and she gets up and walks to the bowl, immediately digging in.

"I guess she considers you her new owner," Mitchell says, crossing his arms as he watches her eat.

I haven't really thought about what will happen to Jezebel in the long run. "I guess that depends on whether or not Elijah is helping Joel. If I'm right and Elijah is innocent in all this, he'll be cleared of charges and Jezebel will be his again."

"And if he's not?" He leans against the kitchen counter.

"I don't know."

Jezebel finishes eating and trots over to sit at my feet.

"She definitely likes you."

I bend down to scratch her chin. "It's mutual," I say.

We're interrupted by a knock on the door.

"Food's here," Mitchell says, going to the front door.

"I'm never going to get rid of him, am I?" I ask Jezebel, who licks my nose.

"Thanks," Mitchell says before closing the door and bringing the food to the kitchen counter. "Eating at the coffee table?" he asks, getting forks and napkins.

"Why not?" I head for the couch since he has the food under control. Jezebel stands next to me, her big eyes pleading for a place on the couch as well. "Oh, come on," I say, and she happily jumps up on the couch and lies down next to me with her head in my lap.

"Well, that happened even sooner than I thought it would," Mitchell says with a smile as he carries our food to the table.

"I'm tired of fighting people pushing their way into my life," I say, leveling him with a look. "I've clearly gotten nowhere with you."

"True."

"Do you do this with all women? Wear them down until they're too tired to protest?" I know he doesn't. Women throw themselves at him.

"Funny," he says, handing me a carton of pork lo mein and a fork.

I immediately twirl the noodles around my fork and take a large mouthful. We eat in silence, both ravished after the long day.

"Any ideas on where Joel is hiding everyone?" he asks.

"Well, after I discovered where Dad was, I thought maybe he was keeping everyone in a different place to prolong our search."

Mitchell nods. "The man is psycho, but he's smart. That would make sense."

"Except I'm not so sure anymore."

"Why not?" Mitchell places his empty container on the

coffee table and repositions so he's facing me with one leg in a figure four on the couch. Jezebel scootches closer to him since I'm still finishing my last bites of food and he's available to rub her belly.

"It's hard to say really. It's more like a feeling. I think he wants Loralei to know the lengths he's going through for her. So he'd want her to know he killed Mindy."

"Because every great romance begins with killing your crush's rival," Mitchell says, rolling his eyes.

"Careful. My eye rolling tendencies are clearly wearing off on you." I point my fork in his direction.

"The horror. Continue. Where do you think he'd take Loralei?"

"If he's really in love with her, like the Phantom was with Christine, he'd bring her somewhere nice."

"Nice but totally exclusive so she's cut off from the rest of the world, right?"

I nod. "'The Music of the Night' mentions leaving behind the world Christine knew. If Joel believes Loralei needs to leave everything behind before she can belong to him, then he'd take her far from Elijah and Weltunkin."

"But if he has Elijah too, he'd have to have them both together somewhere."

"And he was able to kidnap my dad and leave him at Elijah's place, which means he also can't be too far away." I'm missing something. I put my nearly empty container down on the coffee table and rub my forehead. I'm getting yet another headache.

"I'll get you a cold compress for your head. Just lie back and try to relax. It's been a long day."

I cock my head at him. "You know where I keep my cold compress? How much have you looked around this place? You're starting to freak me out."

"I noticed you have one of those cold masks in your refrigerator." He gets up and walks into the kitchen. "Besides, is it really a bad thing that I'm comfortable around you? I don't have to nag you with annoying questions about where things are, and you don't have to wait on me. I'd think you'd be happy about it." He opens the fridge and grabs the mask from the left side door. "Lie down," he says, bringing the mask to me.

I extend my legs, and Jezebel forces herself between the back of the couch and me, her head resting on my stomach. I lean my head on the arm of the couch, and Mitchell places the mask over my eyes.

I'm not sure when it happens, but I drift off to sleep.

A masked man approaches me, his finger beckoning. I look down to see I'm wearing a long white dress. My vision is slightly distorted by the mask on my own face. I open my mouth to speak, to ask this man who he is and where we are, but no words form. I'm speechless.

The place is dark, dimly lit by wall sconces. The open door behind him contains a stairwell leading down. Down to where though? With his eyes locked on mine, he backs down the stairs. As if I can't control my own body, I follow. It's even darker in the stairwell, and I can only feel my surroundings. My hands graze the cold cement walls, and my feet drag along the steps to make sure I don't stumble or trip over the train on my dress.

The man begins to hum, and I recognize the song. It's "The Music of the Night." He's the Phantom. But he doesn't look like the Phantom in the play. This man is different. And somehow, I'm able to see his face alone in the darkness. His mask is black, and his eyes are so dark they appear the same color.

At the bottom of the stairs, we emerge inside a tunnel.

I've never liked tunnels because they make me think of being buried alive, but I can't stop myself from following him. It's like an invisible cord is connecting me to him, forcing me to go where he goes. We walk for several minutes in the narrow tunnel until we reach an opening. It's like a hollowed out cave or something. Stone everywhere. Stalactites and stalagmites nearly meet in the center.

I turn to see a bed and a figure in a white sundress lying across it. She's asleep. No. Not asleep. Drugged? I want to go to her, but I'm unable to leave the Phantom. He stares at her, a smile creeping across his face. Then he meets my gaze and raises a finger to his lips before humming his tune again.

I wake up in a cold sweat and rip the mask from my face. I stare at it. It was the source of my vision-like dream. It connected the clues I've been unable to piece together before now. I sit up and look around. Sunlight is just starting to filter into the room. Mitchell is asleep in the armchair, his neck at an odd angle. Jezebel is curled up at the other end of the couch.

"Mitchell," I say loudly enough to wake him but not so loud as to startle him.

He opens his eyes, and his hand immediately goes to his neck. "Ow." He rubs his neck as he straightens it.

"What are you still doing here?" He should have gone home after I passed out.

Jezebel stirs next to me but doesn't leave the couch.

"I wanted to make sure you were okay. You kept mumbling in your sleep." He sits up straighter, still massaging his cramped neck.

"What did I say?"

"You kept repeating one word: *Phantom*."

I look at the mask in my hands. "I dreamed about him. He led me underground to where he's keeping Loralei."

"You saw Joel in your dream?" He's fully awake now.

"Yeah. I think the reason we can't find him is because he's underground somewhere."

"How is that even possible?" When I don't respond, he adds, "I'm not questioning if you're right. I just don't understand how he'd pull that off."

"He's been free from the psychiatric hospital for a year now. If he's been planning this for a while, he could have found the perfect hiding spot well before he took Loralei." I'm positive he did. He had everything worked out with Mindy's vacation and Loralei's disappearance. This was all premeditated, not a crime of passion thought up in the moment.

"Is he in Weltunkin?" Mitchell asks, leaning forward and resting his forearms on his knees.

I wish I knew. "I think our focus this morning needs to be finding underground places in this city and neighboring towns. Anything. Old bomb shelters. You name it."

"Pennsylvania is famous for steel mines," Mitchell says.

Wrong. My intuition says that while there are mines, that's not the answer here. "I'm getting a firm no on the mines. Scratch those off the list."

"Okay, what about basements in abandoned houses?"

Abandoned. Yes, that's it. "My intuition is buzzing on the word 'abandoned.' Let's start there." I stand up. "I need to take a quick shower before we head to the office."

"Me too. Meet you in half an hour?" He stands up, grabbing his keys off the coffee table.

I nod. "And whatever you do, don't call my dad. He needs a few days off." Though trying to read an article of clothing he wore when Joel took him might give me clues to where Joel was before he kidnapped my father. I could call Mom and discreetly ask for it.

"You're the boss," Mitchell says, grabbing his jacket and heading for the door.

I take a quick shower, feed and walk Jezebel, and call Mom's phone, hoping Dad is still sleeping but knowing the odds aren't good. He's always been an early riser.

"Hi, sweetie. Calling to check on your father?" she asks.

"Yes and also because I need something, but you can't tell him about it."

I hear her footsteps and then a door clicking shut. "Is this for the case?" she whispers.

"Yes. I have an idea where we can find the man who took Dad, but I need something he was wearing when he was taken."

"I threw his clothes in the wash when I woke up this morning. I'm sorry, Piper."

"That's okay." Remembering I still have Dad's ring, I say, "I can use the ring he left in my office for me when he was taken. It helped me find Dad, so it might work now, too. Just take care of him and make sure he gets plenty of rest today. Do not let him try to come to the office."

"He couldn't get past me if he tried," she says, and I can practically hear the smile in her voice.

"Thanks, Mom. Love you."

"Love you, sweetie."

I finish getting ready, say goodbye to Jezebel, and head for the office. Marcia's Nook has a closed sign on the door, which immediately sends up a red flag because she's always open by 6:00 a.m. for those looking to grab coffee before work. I walk up to the door and knock, but there are no lights on. I have her number, so I quickly dial it while still peering inside.

"Piper, hi," Marcia answers.

"Are you okay? I'm standing in front of the store."

"Yes and no. Someone broke into the store last night."

"You were robbed?"

"Looks that way, but the weird thing is nothing is missing. No money was taken because there was none in the register. I'd removed it and deposited it in the bank upon leaving."

"No inventory was missing either?"

"No. Officer Wallace called me when the alarm went off. I came in late last night to check out the place and give a statement, but the police didn't find anything."

That doesn't mean I won't. "Marcia, can I look around your store?"

"Why?"

"I want to see if I can get a read on who did this."

"Okay, but seeing as they didn't take anything, I think they got scared off by the alarm. I doubt they ever even came inside."

"I'll be in my office. Come right in when you get here."

"See you soon," she says before hanging up.

I walk to my office and unlock the door. Stepping inside, I'm greeted by a crinkling sound. I look down to see a piece of paper under my right boot.

I need to talk to you. Meet me at the Weltunkin welcome center at 9:00 a.m.~Elijah

CHAPTER SEVENTEEN

I'm stunned by the note. Elijah was here. And he wants to meet me. But why? And does this mean I was wrong about Joel having him, too?

I bring the piece of paper to my desk, where I remove my jacket and place my purse in the bottom drawer. This is the only thing of Elijah's that I have at the moment, so I'm going to have to hope it's enough to get a read off of.

I press my right palm to the paper. The vision is anything but clear. Glimpses of Elijah.

Scribbling the note while standing at my door.

Hearing something like footsteps.

Breaking into Marcia's Nook.

Frantic. Trying to hide. Fear courses through him.

I pick up my hand. Elijah was scared. He broke into Marcia's Nook with one thought on his mind. Hiding. From Joel?

"Hey," Mitchell says, walking in the door. "I heard about Marcia's. Have you talked to her?"

I nod. "It was Elijah who broke in." I pick up the paper and hold it out to him. "After leaving this for me."

Mitchell reads the paper and then consults his watch. "I'm going with you."

I figured as much. "Marcia's on her way here. I told her I'd help her find who broke in."

"Call her. Then we can leave for the welcome center and figure out what the hell is going on."

I grab my phone from my purse and dial Marcia. "Hey, you don't need to come. I figured out who did it, and Detective Brennan is aware. The man wasn't trying to steal anything. He was hiding from someone the police are looking for."

"Is it safe for me to open the store today?"

I put my hand over the phone and whisper, "Can she open today?"

Mitchell nods. "I'll get someone to watch the place."

I remove my hand. "You're good. Detective Brennan will have someone keep an eye on the store."

"Thank you. And tell him I said thank you as well."

"I will. Be safe. You know we have security here in the strip mall. You should call them and make sure they're aware of the break-in. I'm sure they'll keep a closer eye on the place if you do."

"Good idea." She pauses. "Piper?"

I know what she's going to ask, but I wait for her to say it.

"Does the break-in have to do with one of your cases?"

"Yes. I'm sorry, Marcia. I never meant for my job and the proximity of my office to your store to cause problems for you." I rub my forehead.

"Sweetie, this is not your fault. I just want to tell you to be safe. I know how you like to take care of yourself, but keep Detective Brennan close, at least until this case is over."

I raise my gaze to Mitchell. "I'll be safe. Don't worry." I hang up.

"Her place is broken into and she's worried about you," Mitchell says.

"See. I told you she's too good for you." I smirk and grab my jacket and purse. "You driving?" We need to leave now if we're going to meet Elijah on time.

"Let's do this," Mitchell says, already starting for the door.

The Weltunkin welcome center isn't packed, but there are plenty of people around. I'm assuming that's why Elijah wanted to meet here. Maybe he thinks Joel won't be able to grab him with witnesses around.

"What's the verdict on Elijah?" Mitchell asks as we scan the crowd. "Do you trust him, or do you think he set this up on Joel's behalf?"

"He was clearly afraid of Joel finding him, so I'm pretty sure he's looking for my help."

"*Our* help," he corrects me.

"Right."

The men's room door opens, and Elijah peeks out.

"Over there," I say. "Men's room." I head for it with Mitchell matching my every step.

Elijah sees us and looks all around. Is he trying to figure out if we brought backup? He casually walks over to a rack with brochures for local attractions and restaurants. He picks one up and pretends to read it.

I move in next to him and do the same.

"I wasn't sure you'd come," he says.

"How could I not? Does Joel know you're here?"

"I wouldn't be talking to you right now if he did." He puts the brochure back and picks up another. "I got away."

"I see that. Were you with Loralei?"

"No. He wouldn't take me to her. Smart on his part. She'd probably be with me now if he had."

"Then where did he take you?" I eye Mitchell, who is pretending to look at something on his phone. Or maybe he's recording the conversation.

"I went to his place, but he wasn't there. So I went to our childhood home."

Why didn't I think to check there? Joel grew up in that house. And considering his parents sent him away, I'm sure he'd associate that place with a lot of bad memories. He could be trying to reclaim the house in some sick way. "Are your parents still alive?"

"No. My father had a heart attack two years ago, and my mother was an alcoholic. She couldn't handle locking up Joel for all those years. She died long before Joel was released."

"The house is still there, though?"

"Yeah, it's there. No one has bought it. The rumors surrounding the place got out of hand after Joel was released. I guess Realtors have to disclose certain information. Joel had tortured and killed animals in the basement. No one wants to buy a place where a psychotic kid grew up."

"Why didn't you mention your brother when I told you Loralei was missing?"

"I had no idea he was behind this at first. But when I went to pick up Jezebel and found out Joel was supposedly on vacation, I knew I had to find out."

"He tried to kill your dog," I say.

"No." Elijah's voice rises, making several people turn in our direction. "Leah is supposed to be watching her."

"He paid Leah a visit."

"Is she...?"

"She's fine. He took the house key from her and locked my father in a dog crate in your basement. I think he wanted to frame you for Loralei's disappearance."

"Where's Jez?"

"My father is fine. Thanks for asking." I scoff and shake my head. "Jezebel is with me. I'll take care of her until this is all over."

Elijah is quiet for several moments. "I don't know where Loralei is or even if she's still alive. My brother is unhinged. I'm not sure what he's capable of."

"Are you aware of his fascination with *The Phantom of the Opera*?"

"The Broadway show?" He shakes his head. "Our parents went to see it when we were kids, but Joel stayed home with me. Why?"

"Never mind. Do you have any idea where he might have Loralei?"

"You read things, right? That's how you solve crimes. So I brought you something." He reaches into his pocket, which makes Mitchell's hand lower to his hip where his gun is holstered. Elijah pulls a pocket watch from his jacket. "It's Joel's. It belonged to our mother's father before him, but Joel always had it with him." He extends his hand to me, and I'm careful to take it with my left hand, not wanting to get a vision right here in front of everyone.

"Thank you. You should come to the police station with us. We can protect you until we find Joel."

Elijah looks back and forth between Mitchell and me. "No offense, but I don't think you guys can protect me if Joel wants me dead."

"Do you have reason to think he does?" Mitchell asks, speaking up for the first time.

"When he was released, I tried to help him. I even let

him list me as a reference so he could get a job. I told myself he was cured." He runs a hand through his already messy hair. "I was wrong. He wasn't cured. He was plotting his revenge."

"On you?" I ask.

"On all of us."

"You said your parents are dead," Mitchell says. "Who else does that leave?"

"Everyone you care about," I say to Joel. "Mindy, Loralei, and even Jezebel."

"Why would he hate you?" Mitchell asks. "You tried to help him."

"I don't know. But when I caught up to him, the way he looked at me... It was pure hatred in his eyes."

"Then you need to come with us to the station. Let us protect you," Mitchell says.

Elijah is quiet for a minute, and then he nods. "Okay. Let me use the restroom first, though."

I eye him suspiciously, not sure if this is a trick. My intuition says he's telling the truth. He's terrified of his brother, and while he doesn't truly believe we can keep him safe, he knows he's better off with us than on his own. I nod to Mitchell, who steps aside to let him pass.

We keep an eye on the restroom door while Elijah is inside.

"What do you think?" Mitchell asks. "Is he hiding anything?"

I squeeze the pocket watch in my left hand. "He wouldn't have given me this if he was. He's scared. Really scared."

The minutes pass while we watch the door. Finally, Mitchell says, "I'm going in. Stay here." His hand is on his hip, ready in case Elijah puts up a fight. Not that I think he would. He opens the bathroom door slowly and looks around before stepping inside. I scan the rest of the welcome center. In the corner by the large window, a family of four poses for a picture. Thanks to the celebrities who like to vacation here, we get a lot of tourists. That and we have indoor water parks and ski lodges that draw crowds in the winter.

The door to the men's room opens, and Mitchell steps out alone.

"Where is he?" I ask, hurrying over to Mitchell.

"Gone. There's no one in there."

"How is that possible? We were watching the door the entire time." I look around, even though I know Elijah didn't come back out here.

"I don't know," Mitchell says, frustration evident in his voice.

"You said the restroom is empty, right?" I ask.

He nods. "Why?"

"I'm going in. Cover me. Don't let anyone inside."

He puts his hand on my arm. "Piper, what are you going to do?"

"Try to get a read off the room to determine what happened in there."

He gestures to the pocket watch still in my left hand. "Maybe you should try to read that."

I've been afraid to. Seeing into Joel's mind is going to be awful. So awful I'll most likely need to be in the privacy of my own home, not in a disgusting public restroom. "Not here. Not unless it's a last resort."

His expression softens. "Maybe we should just go then. Elijah probably went out the window to get away from us."

"No. He's afraid of his brother. I could tell. I think he wants our protection."

"Then what happened to him? Joel couldn't possibly have been in there waiting for him. He has to be with Loralei, right?"

I lift the pocket watch. "We'll know soon enough. Right now, I have to get inside that bathroom." I step past him, giving him a quick glance over my shoulder before shutting myself inside. Sometimes the looks Mitchell gives me are overwhelming. I'm not sure he sees me at all in moments like this. Being around me can't be easy for him since I remind him so much of his mother.

The restroom is empty like Mitchell said. There are four stalls with green doors along one wall. The window he mentioned is between the stalls and the row of sinks on the other end of the bathroom. I walk between the stalls and urinals to the window, knowing Elijah touched it to escape. I just need to find out why.

The thought of touching anything in here disgusts me, but I reach up and place my right hand on the window latch. I take a deep breath and close my eyes.

Elijah is standing in front of the mirrors, staring at his phone vibrating in his hand. Joel's name pops up on the caller ID. He shakes his head. "No. I'm not going to answer you." He ignores the call, letting it go to voice mail. A few seconds later, a text message pops up on the screen, making Elijah jump with the vibration of the notification.

Joel: If you go to the police, I'll kill her. Meet me where we used to play as kids. Come alone, or so help me, I'll gut her alive and make you watch.

Elijah squeezes the phone in his fist and stifles the urge to scream. He turns toward the door and then changes direction completely, going for the window instead.

An image of a mausoleum appears and quickly fades away.

I let go of the window latch and walk out of the restroom. Mitchell has a questioning look on his face. I motion toward the exit so we can talk in the car. I already have an idea of where we need to go.

We get into the Explorer, but Mitchell doesn't start the engine. He swivels in the seat to face me.

"Joel contacted Elijah. He threatened to kill Loralei if Elijah didn't meet him where they played as kids, which I'm guessing is a cemetery, considering I saw a glimpse of a mausoleum."

"Then it has to be the Weltunkin Cemetery, right? It has several mausoleums, and Elijah and Joel grew up here."

"Agreed. I don't know if we'll find them in time, but let's head there."

Mitchell starts the car and backs out of the parking spot.

"Oh, and I saw the number Joel called from. I don't remember it off hand, but if I can recall the image, I think I could read it."

"The last time you recalled a vision, you had to mimic the sound of rain. Were there any noises you could mimic this time?" He pulls onto the highway.

"No. But maybe being in a bathroom near a sink would be enough. I'm not sure."

"Having his phone number could mean tracing the phone," Mitchell says as if I didn't already think of that.

"I'll do my best."

"I didn't mean to imply you weren't already," he says, glancing at me briefly.

"I know." No one ever comes out and says it or means to make me feel bad, but I know they all wish I'd see more. Hell, I wish it, too.

Mitchell turns into the cemetery. The gates are situated on flat land, but the cemetery itself contains several rolling hills. It's also huge, which means going on foot will cost us precious time, allowing Joel and Elijah to sneak away. But driving draws attention. There really is no good option.

"What kind of kids play in a cemetery?" Mitchell asks.

"Joel tortured and killed animals. Now he's taken at least one human life. Maybe his obsession with death started here," I offer. And then another thought comes to me. "Their parents are dead. What if one of the mausoleums is a family mausoleum?"

"We have no choice but to drive," Mitchell says. "We can't search them all on foot before Joel gets away, and we have no idea which mausoleum belongs to their family."

I nod. Mitchell is armed. If we spot Joel, Mitchell could order him to stop. What happens after that is entirely up to Joel's desire to live.

The first mausoleum we come to has the name Shubert on it, so we keep driving.

"Are we looking for Graham or Wood?" Mitchell asks.

"Graham," I say with so much conviction we both know I'm right.

We reach the back end of the cemetery, and I hone in on a mausoleum. "There!" I point to it, my hand on the door handle, ready to jump out as soon as Mitchell stops the car.

He drives closer before cutting the engine, and we both jump out. I can read the name engraved on the front: Graham. Mitchell draws his gun as we approach. He puts his hand on the mausoleum door and gives me a nod before throwing the door open and yelling, "Nobody move!"

I look inside at the empty mausoleum. "I'm pretty sure they can't move," I say, following Mitchell inside. "Considering the only other people in here besides us are dead."

"Damn it!" Mitchell puts his gun away. "Maybe they were never here."

I move to examine something on the edge of the windowsill. "Oh, they were here. And Joel definitely took Elijah." I pick up the phone and smile. "But Elijah left me a present so I'd find him."

CHAPTER EIGHTEEN

Mitchell walks over to me with a huge smile on his face. "Looks like you don't have to try to recall Joel's number now either. I'm so happy I could kiss you."

I level him with a look, and he holds up his hands between us.

"Don't worry. It's just an expression. I know better than to try that."

"Good. Besides, Elijah is the one you should kiss. He left this here."

"True, but let's forget I mentioned kissing anyone." He cocks his head. "How would Elijah know you'd find the phone?"

"I guess he believes in my abilities." Or, more likely, it was an act of desperation.

"Let me grab Joel's phone number and make a call to get its location traced."

I hand him the phone, but he curses when he can't get past the lock screen. "Now what?"

I hold out my right hand. "That's child's play."

He places the phone in my hand and watches me. I take

a deep breath and close my eyes, focusing on Elijah unlocking the phone. Luckily, it's an older iPhone, so it doesn't use facial recognition. All I need is a passcode. The number comes to me easily, and I type it in. "There," I say, handing the phone back to Mitchell.

"Thank you." He presses the icon for recent calls. Joel is at the top of the list. One touch of the information icon and Mitchell has Joel's phone number. He types it into his own phone and saves the contact. "Here. Hang on to this. See if you can get anything else off it while I call the station."

"You get all the easy jobs," I say, taking the phone again.

He rolls his eyes as he walks to the other side of the mausoleum to make his call.

I've been taxing my abilities a lot the past few days, but reading Elijah's phone seems a lot better than reading Joel's pocket watch. I focus on the phone and the moment Elijah met Joel here, but something else comes to my mind instead.

Joel frantically paces the small bedroom. His childhood bedroom. The walls are a faded blue with baseball wall trim running around the top of the room. "Our entire lives, you've had everything! It's my turn. My turn to get the girl of my dreams."

"She's not the girl of your dreams. She's the girl of my dreams, you lunatic!" Elijah is tied up on the floor.

Joel hauls off and slaps Elijah across the face. "Shut up! You don't get to call me that. I've been denied the opportunity to ever get close to a woman because I've been locked up and medicated."

"That was your doing. I begged you to stop, but you kept torturing any living creature you could get your hands on. How many bodies are buried in that backyard?"

"I'm curious about life and death. They were all strays and wild animals. It's not like I took someone's pet."

"How did you even find out about Loralei?" Elijah asks. "I never told you about her. I made sure I didn't."

"Computer time for good behavior. I was the model patient. Just as Dr. Martinson said, I'm perfectly capable of being"—he makes air quotes—"'a fully functional member of society.'" He throws his head back and laughs. "Fooling him was almost too easy. And he thought I was interested in you because I wanted to reconnect with my family. Totally normal reaction for a sane person. I wanted to know all about my beloved half brother, Elijah. I read all about your marriage and divorce to Mindy. If you ask me, I did you a huge favor by killing her. No more alimony payments for you. You should be thanking me. Letting me have Loralei isn't too much to ask in return."

"You kidnapped her. Did you expect me to sit around and let you harm her?"

"I wasn't planning to harm her at all. I was planning to love her. To give her everything you couldn't."

"How do you know I couldn't?"

"She married someone else. All because you weren't good for her. She knew that."

"Did she tell you that?"

"She told me a lot of things. Not that she needed to. I've been watching her. Did you know Mindy threatened her? Even after your divorce. Do you want to know why your ex-wife was such a bitch to you, Elijah?" He leans down in Elijah's face. "Because she still loved your sorry ass. If not for Loralei, she'd still be your wife. In fact, when I first met Mindy, she tried to persuade me to kill Loralei for her, clearing her path back to you."

"What?"

"But I couldn't do it. Call it love at first sight, but I was already hooked on Loralei, and I certainly couldn't *allow Mindy to hire someone else to kill the woman I loved."*

When the vision fades, I'm breathing heavily. Mitchell is off the phone now, and he moves toward me.

"I saw Elijah tied up in Joel's childhood bedroom."

"Now?" His eyes widen, hoping I have a current location.

"No." I swallow hard. "It was from when he first confronted Joel. Joel told Elijah Mindy hired him to kill Loralei because she wrecked their marriage. Mindy was still in love with Elijah."

"So Mindy orchestrated all of this?"

One thought keeps swirling around in my mind. *How many bodies are buried in that backyard?* I meet Mitchell's gaze. "No. Joel is responsible for everything. He thinks he's in love with Loralei, and he couldn't let Mindy harm her."

"So you're saying Joel killed Mindy?"

"Yes, and I know where Mindy's body is buried."

———

Twenty-five minutes later, we're on the other side of town in the driveway of a Victorian gray colonial with black shutters. The "For Sale" sign on the lawn doesn't seem to be doing much good for this place.

"How is Joel getting past the lockbox on the front door?" Mitchell asks as we exit his Explorer.

My dream about Joel leading me down into a tunnel pops into my head. Only this time I'm going to go up. "The basement. He's going in through the basement door."

We walk around to the back of the house. Under the back deck is a basement door. Like I suspected, the door is unlocked, and Mitchell turns the knob with ease. He has his gun in hand just in case.

We step into the basement, the only light coming in through the door behind us. I reach for the light switch on the wall to my right, but Mitchell shakes his head. He doesn't want to alert Joel we're here. Of course, the Explorer in the driveway already lets anyone nearby know someone is here. Still, I take my phone from my back pocket, having left my purse in the car, and use the flashlight feature to light our way once I shut the door behind us.

We walk through the empty basement, which is divided into three areas, one of which appears to be for doing laundry based on the water hookups. The stairs are carpeted, muffling our steps as we climb. We reach the door at the top, and Mitchell opens it just enough to peek through the small crevice. Satisfied no one is nearby, he opens the door fully and steps into the mudroom.

The energy inside the house is a mixture of angst and fear. I shudder and wrap my arms around myself. Mitchell eyes me, but I shake my head. There's no time to stop and discuss my feelings. We need to keep searching.

We go through the kitchen and living room to the stair-well. I motion up it. It was Joel's bedroom I saw in the vision, so that's where I want to go. No matter what awful energy is waiting for me there. At the top of the stairs, I motion to the right. The door at the end of the hall is practically pulsing with energy. I place my left hand on the wall to steady myself as I walk toward the door.

Mitchell stops walking and whispers in my ear, "Can you sense him on the other side of that door?"

I shake my head. "He's not here anymore."

Mitchell presses a finger to his lips anyway and advances on the door. He flings it open, gun poised in front of him. But just like with the mausoleum, the room is empty. I take a tentative step inside, and my knees buckle on me.

"Piper." Mitchell rushes to me, catching me before I fall. He holsters his gun and peers down into my eyes.

"He...he's full of so much hatred." Tears stream down my cheeks, and Mitchell continues to cradle me in his arms. I'm not surprised Joel ended up in a psychiatric hospital. No one could survive with this much rage inside them. But what caused it? Why was he so angry at everyone?

Mitchell's phone rings, but he doesn't move to answer it.

"Get it," I say. "It could be important." I stagger to my feet again so he can answer the call.

"Brennan," he says, placing the call on speaker now that he knows we're alone in the house.

"We've got a location on the phone number you gave us."

"Great. Hit me with it."

"The last known location that phone made a call from was Trinity Street in Weltunkin."

"More specifically 229 Trinity Street," I say.

"That's where we are now," Mitchell says. "He's not here. Thanks for checking it out, though. Did the service provider say if the phone is still on?"

"It's been shut off."

"My guess is he ditched it when he realized Elijah didn't have his phone anymore," I say, still using the wall for support.

"Thanks," Mitchell says into the phone before disconnecting the call. He pockets the phone and reaches for me, but I wave him away.

"I'm okay."

"No, you're not. You have to let me help you, Piper. This can't all be on you."

"Then look around. Find some clues while I do my thing." I don't mean to snap at him, but I hate being coddled.

"Is that what you'd tell your father if he were here?"

"Believe me when I say I'd love to, but he's not here because of Joel. So let's focus on finding that bastard."

"What about Mindy's body? You said she was buried here somewhere." He looks around.

"If you're expecting to find her sitting in a rocking chair like Norman Bates's mother, you watch too many horror movies." I jerk my thumb behind me. "She's buried in the backyard. Call Wallace to bring Harry in to locate her."

"On it." He gets his phone out again and makes the call.

Since the room is empty of furniture, I have nothing to read but the walls, floor, and window. But I do have Joel's pocket watch. Though trying to read it here with all this negative energy already bogging me down is near suicidal. My purpose here has to be recovering Mindy's body.

"They're on their way," Mitchell says.

"Good. Then we're finished here."

"What?" He couldn't look more stunned.

"I can't work in these conditions. I'm struggling to stay on my feet. If I read anything here, it could put me out of commission for days."

He knows better than to argue with me. "Let's go. We'll get you home. You probably need to check on Jezebel anyway."

I nod. Having a dog is definitely going to change my daily routine.

Mitchell calls Officer Wallace on our way back to my

place and lets him know we've left. He also stops at Matty's sub shop to get us lunch.

Jezebel greets me with several licks to my face and a tail that's wagging so fast and hard it thumps against everything nearby, including the kitchen chair.

"You thirsty?" I ask her, already filling her bowl with water.

"Are dogs easier to read than humans?" Mitchell asks, bringing our sandwiches to the coffee table.

"Yes, mostly because they're much purer souls." I pet Jezebel's head while she drinks. "They don't try to hide their feelings."

"Makes sense. I had a friend whose cat used to poop on his pillow every time he left for college. I'd say the cat's feelings about Dante leaving were clear." He laughs as he sits down to eat.

I grab some napkins and two bottles of water from the refrigerator before joining Mitchell on the couch. Jezebel follows, taking the spot between Mitchell and me.

"Do you think she did this to Elijah and Mindy when they were married?" Mitchell asks, gesturing to Jez.

"Possibly. Or maybe she senses the distance between us and knows she can fill that space."

"What, the dog is psychic now, too?"

I roll my eyes. "You don't need to be psychic to tell two people aren't in a relationship." I unwrap my Italian sub and take a big bite. "You remembered extra banana pepper rings," I say with my mouth full.

"You know, you're right. It's easy to see we aren't together. Just as easy as it is to see your chewed sandwich in your mouth when you speak."

I turn in his direction and open my mouth wide.

"So attractive, Piper."

I shrug and continue eating.

Once Mitchell is finished with his sub, he crumples up the wrapper and downs the rest of his water. Then he sits back, one arm draped over the couch. "When are we going to discuss what you felt back at that house?"

"We're not. I didn't get a vision, so there's not much to tell."

"You didn't want to have a vision. I've never seen you so scared to read someone."

I place the rest of my sub on the table and pick up my water bottle. "Not that any of the criminals I've gotten reads on have been the picture of sanity, but the vibe I'm getting from Joel is particularly scary."

"How can I help?"

Jezebel must sense my unease because she puts her head in my lap. I pet her, letting the repetitive action of running my hand over the top of her head calm my nerves.

"I'm getting the feeling the dog is able to help you more than I am," Mitchell says.

"Sorry, but you're not entirely incorrect. She calms me."

"Maybe you should consider getting a dog when this is all over."

I haven't given much thought to having to return Jezebel to Elijah. She's not my dog, whether I—and possibly she—want her to be. "Joel's pocket watch is in the left pocket of my jacket. Would you get it for me?"

"The dog gets to relax while I play fetch. Real nice." He gets up and goes to my jacket, which is hanging on the hook behind the front door. He studies the watch as he brings it to me. "This thing is old. How do you know you won't get a vision about Joel's grandfather instead?"

"I'm going to focus on Joel specifically." I hold out my hand, but lower it again when I notice Mitchell is squeezing the pocket watch in his right hand. "Are you trying to read it?" I ask.

He huffs and turns the watch over in his hand. "I thought maybe...since my mom..." He hands it to me. "It was stupid."

"No it's not." I take the watch in my left hand. "I get that you want to understand it better because of her. There's no shame in that." In moments like this, I wish I were a medium so I could tell Mitchell how his mother is doing. Give him some peace of mind. "We can't change the past, though. And I don't think your mom would want you to even if you could."

He shakes his head. "It's fine. Let's focus on the case." He sits down and pets Jezebel. Maybe he finds her calming, too. "What are you hoping to see in the vision?"

"Loralei. Her location. That's it." I don't want to stay in the vision too long and see inside Joel's mind. Nor do I want to see how he killed Mindy.

"Good luck. I'll be right here. Jezebel, too."

As if she understands, Jezebel climbs onto my lap and stares up at me. "Sure. I'm a chair now," I say.

Mitchell smiles, seeming more at ease than a few moments ago.

I take several deep breaths to center myself. "I think I'm as ready as I'm going to be," I say, giving Mitchell one last glance before placing the pocket watch in my right hand.

Elijah is on the ground someplace so dark it's difficult to see much of anything but stone. "Please, Joel. Just don't hurt her. Let her go. She doesn't need to be part of all this."

"You made her a part of this. It all traces back to you, Elijah. All of it. You were the good son. The perfect one. Good grades in school. Popular. Athletic. Mom and Dad

were so proud of you. That was my life until you came along."

"That wasn't my fault."

"You don't think it's your fault that I was tossed aside? You were born on my birthday! What are the odds of that? That day, it was like I died. Your father was going to adopt me until you came along. Then I became nothing more than the stepson. I was the difficult birth that nearly killed Mom, while you were the uncomplicated C-section. I had croup while you slept through the night from the start. When I cried, Dad backhanded me. When you cried, Mom coddled you."

"Joel, I had no control over what either of them did. They were shitty parents to you. I get it."

"And you were a shitty brother! You wanted me locked up just as much as they did. I heard you all talking that night. Heard you all agree that you'd all be better off without me."

"That's not what we said. We agreed you needed help."

Joel laughs. "Help. Well, I got help. I learned to help myself to all the things life denied me. Like Loralei. She's all the help I need."

"No. Please, Joel. I love her. She loves me."

"She might now, but that will change. Believe me it will. She'll learn to love me, or she'll pay with her life. Just like everyone else in this family. Mom and Dad's deaths wound up being helpful in so many ways in the end."

"Please don't. I'm begging you."

"But there's something I need to take care of before Loralei can become mine. One obstacle left in my way." He bends down and peers into Elijah's eyes. "I had planned to pin Mindy's murder on you. With you in a jail cell for life, Loralei would have to move on. But you went and ruined that by talking to that private investigator and her detective friend. You really leave me with no other choice, dear brother."

"Joel, please."

"You almost ruined everything. I created this place for Loralei, and now she won't even be able to enjoy it thanks to you. Once she sees your dead body, we'll need to leave. Leave before that psychic hound comes sniffing me out."

"I can get them off your trail. Leave Loralei and just run. I won't know where you're going, so they'll never get anything out of me. You can start over."

Joel cocks his head as if considering Elijah's plan. "You never were as smart as I am." He reaches inside his jacket and pulls out a knife, which he thrusts into Elijah's stomach.

CHAPTER NINETEEN

I'm screaming, and Jezebel is barking directly in my face. Mitchell tries to pull her off me, but I reach for her, wrapping my arms around her neck and hugging her. She lets me hold her without trying to break free. When I finally let go, she licks my wet cheeks.

"You were trying to break me out of the vision, weren't you?" I ask her. "Did you sense what happened?" I take her face in my hands. "I'm so sorry, baby girl, but it looks like you're going to be stuck with me."

"Are you saying Elijah is dead?" Mitchell asks.

I nod. "I saw Joel kill him." My gaze lowers to the pocket watch beside me on the couch. "Please take that away."

Mitchell scoops it up and places it in his pocket. "Piper, I know you're still recovering, but I need to know what else you saw. Is Loralei alive?"

"Yes. Joel said he won't hurt her as long as she loves him. He said Elijah was the last thing standing in the way of her loving him."

"So he killed his brother to get the girl." Mitchell runs a hand through his hair. "Did you see where they were?"

"All I saw was stone. It was too dark."

"The mausoleum?" He starts pacing in front of the coffee table.

"No. It's not dark out."

He stops and faces me. "Wait. You think you were seeing things as they were actually happening?"

"It felt that way. And Joel plans to take Loralei and leave, which means we're running out of time. We have to find her now, or we may never find her."

"I hate to do this, but what else can you tell me, Piper? I'm going into this blind."

"He thinks his mother's and stepfather's deaths were karma or something. That the universe killed them because of what they did to him."

"Which was what?"

I shrug. "Played favorites. He told Elijah their parents basically stopped caring about him once Elijah was born."

"That hardly seems like enough to drive someone crazy to the point of killing people."

"You never know what can set a person off." I stroke Jezebel's head, which is in my lap again. "I swear she knows."

"Are you going to keep her?" Mitchell asks.

"I think it would be good for both of us. I don't want to see her wind up in a shelter."

"All right, let's go over what we know about where Joel could have Loralei. You think it's underground, right?"

"Yeah. Did the Weltunkin PD get you a list of bomb shelters in the area?"

"They did, but I have another idea." He sits down again. "Their research turned up something else that I want to run by you. Let me know if you get any pings from your intuition on this."

"Hit me," I say.

"There used to be a subway system that ran under the city. They shut it down back in the fifties after a cave-in killed hundreds of people."

Tingles run down my spine. "That's it. That's why we walked down stairs in my dream. It's a subway system."

"Okay, but here's the problem. They filled it in."

"All of it? That would take a lot of cement. Why not just close in the entrances and the part that caved in?"

"It's possible they did, but let's say that's true. How do we find where Joel is accessing the subway system?"

It needs to be somewhere no one else would notice. "I need to see a map of the subway system. Something might jump out at me."

"I can pull one up online."

Jezebel whines, letting me know she needs to go out.

"You do that while I walk Jez." I stand, but Mitchell holds up his hand to stop me.

"I'm not sure you should go outside alone right now. You're unsteady from all the visions, and Joel knows you're after him. Until we have him, I don't like the idea of you being alone outside."

"I didn't realize you'd become my bodyguard," I say. "I'll be fine. Jez will be with me."

"Joel has already encountered Jezebel, remember? What makes you think she'd scare him off now?"

"Fine. Her leash is on the chair in the kitchen." I pet Jezebel on the head. "You be good for Mitchell, okay?"

She licks me before following Mitchell to the door.

I get my phone and pull up a map of the old subway system. It ran under the entire city. The collapse occurred near the Main Street entrance. My guess is that entrance is fully sealed now. They would have filled it with cement. I scroll until I find a map that shows the entire city in one shot. It's too small to read the names of the stops, but that's okay. I just need to pinpoint a location.

"That's odd," I say aloud to myself. One of the entrances looks like it's near the cemetery, but that can't be right. Why would a subway stop be located by a cemetery?

Mitchell returns with Jezebel pulling him through the door to come see me. She gives one sharp bark for my attention.

"Were you a good girl?" I ask her.

"She was," Mitchell says, removing her leash. "Find anything?"

"Maybe. Look at this."

Jezebel jumps up as if I'm talking to her.

Mitchell peers around her at my phone screen. "The cemetery?"

"What if the reason Joel knew about the subway system is because he found an entrance to it years ago while playing in the cemetery?"

"So you think he came back here with the perfect location to kidnap Loralei already planned out." It's not a question because he can see exactly where I'm going with this.

"He had a year to plot this. A year to dig out an entrance to the subway tunnels and create that underground world for him and Loralei."

"That makes sense, but how does he access it? We were at the cemetery, and we didn't see an entrance to the subway tunnel."

Something from my vision comes to mind. "Joel told Elijah that their parents' deaths were helpful in many ways."

"Joel never had to see them after he got out of the hospital, so that's one way."

"What if the other way was the fact that they had a mausoleum built?"

"You think the entrance to the subway is in the mausoleum?"

"Not the real entrance. But the one Joel created, yes."

"That means we might have missed them by seconds in the cemetery."

"The question now is did Joel create more than one entrance?" If he didn't, we could ambush him as long as he hasn't already taken Loralei and left.

"He's smart, so there's a good chance he did, but more than one entrance would mean more than one way for Loralei to escape."

"So maybe not," I say. "He wants Loralei. He thinks the world owes him, and for whatever reason, he's chosen her as his prize."

"I'm calling for backup."

"Not my dad," I say. "Leave him out of this."

"Piper, he's left me three voice mails. I just listened to them while I was walking Jez. I have to tell him something."

"Why? You're not his partner anymore. What is he going to do to you?"

"You've met your dad, right? The guy can be scary."

I stand up and clap him on the side of his shoulder. "Woman up."

"Um, I think you mean 'man up.'"

"No, I mean 'woman up.' Women are much stronger than men. Smarter too, but we don't have time to argue. We need to get to that mausoleum and find Loralei before it's too late."

"Do you believe this, Jez?" Mitchell asks as I grab my jacket.

She gives a sharp bark.

"You tell him, Jez. Sorry, Mitchell, but you're outnumbered." I open the door, and Mitchell follows me out.

He calls for backup on the way but refrains from using the flashing light to get us to the cemetery quicker. We keep a constant look out for Joel in case he's already left the subway system and is taking Loralei somewhere. My guess is he'd steal a car. Probably from someone parked in or near the cemetery. I scan every car we pass but don't see him anywhere. That's good. It means we might be in time.

We beat the other officers to the mausoleum, which is also good. Since we don't know if there's another exit, I don't want to go into the tunnel guns blazing. I want to sneak up on him so that Mitchell can get a clear shot at him when he doesn't come quietly—because I know he won't. He'll go down swinging and try to take us out with him.

Mitchell has his gun raised as he opens the door to the mausoleum. Since we didn't see the entrance to the subway system the last time we were here, I know it's hidden.

"Why couldn't this be the movies? Then there would be a big coffin in the center of the room that opened up to reveal stairs," Mitchell says.

"I'm going to pretend you didn't say that." I look around. The wall containing the bodies is thick enough to conceal an entrance to the subway, but how do I try to open it? I press on the nameplates for each of Joel's parents, but nothing happens.

"Wait. My idea was stupid, but you're pressing on bricks to see if they open a secret door? You're a Scooby-Doo lover, aren't you?"

"Who isn't?" I say, continuing to look. "Now help me."

Mitchell bends down. "There's room for other coffins here under the parents."

Or... I bend down too, running my hand across the stone. One of them feels warm. "I can feel energy coming from this one," I say. "It has to mean the entrance has something to do with this stone in particular." I press my right palm flat against it.

Another hand fills my vision. Joel's hand. He pushes the stone, and it slides back slightly. His hand moves upward, and his index finger finds a latch that releases the door to the bottom two shelf spaces. Each is the width of a coffin, but the height is double that, almost like it's meant to house four coffins.

I push the stone, sliding it back, and unlatch the bottom compartment the way I saw Joel do.

"Whoa," Mitchell says as he looks into the opening inside. "It's like crawling into a grave."

"He's obsessed with death, remember?"

I stare into the blackness. In my dream, I opened a door and descended stairs. Now, I opened a drawer and am going to descend into the darkness to find the tunnel leading to Loralei. My heart pounds in anticipation.

"Let me go first. I'm the one who's armed," Mitchell says. "Think there are stairs?"

"Probably more like a downward sloping tunnel until we reach the subway system below."

Mitchell ducks his head and steps into the tunnel. I use my phone to light our way so he can keep his gun trained in front of us. The ground slopes downward before turning into a tunnel. The tunnel is narrow, just like in my dream, but that makes sense considering Joel had to dig this out himself.

A thought strikes me, and I tap Mitchell on the shoulder. He stops and leans his head toward me while still keeping his eyes and gun directed in front of us.

"I saw Elijah murdered down here. His body must be in this tunnel."

Mitchell nods.

I have to add Elijah's name to the list of people my abilities couldn't save. Not that I think I'm meant to save everyone, but it still hurts. Elijah Graham wasn't a saint by any means, but he didn't deserve to die, especially at the hands of his mentally unstable brother. Elijah tried to save Loralei in the end, and I'm sure he knew he could lose his life in the process.

The metallic smell in the air alerts us to Elijah's body before it comes into view. Mitchell holds up his hand, indicating I should stay where I am. But he can't shield me from this. I saw Joel stab Elijah. I experienced it in my vision, and there is no way to get around the body in this cramped tunnel without getting a good glimpse of it, even in the dark.

Mitchell bends down. I assume to check for a pulse, but I'm trying not to look too closely. I know he's dead. I'm sure Mitchell knows it too, but he's trained to follow certain procedures anyway. He stands up and reaches his hand back to me, to help guide me over the body.

I can't stop myself from looking when I step over the body. Elijah's head is propped up against the wall. His eyes open and vacant. I communicate a silent apology for not saving him, and then I turn away. Loralei can still be saved, and that's what Elijah would want me to focus on.

We walk a little ways before we see an opening up ahead. Mitchell chances a look over his shoulder at me, and I nod for him to continue. This is it. Loralei is still here. I can feel it.

At the opening, Mitchell peeks around, looking for signs

of Joel. Unlike in my dream, there are no stalagmites and stalactites. Instead, there are cement beams that used to be part of the subway tunnels. It doesn't look like the Phantom's underground dwelling either. I guess my imagination filled in what my intuition didn't know at the time. The concept is still the same, though. Joel intended to keep Loralei here, secluded from everyone she knows. He wanted her all to himself. Too bad Mitchell and I are about to ruin those plans for good. Joel is going to live a secluded life, but it won't be down here.

"Right on time," Joel says, stepping out of the shadows with a lantern in one hand and gun in the other.

CHAPTER TWENTY

"Drop your weapon," Mitchell yells, but Joel doesn't even flinch.

"You waited for us," I say. "Why?"

Mitchell's brow furrows, but he doesn't dare take his eyes or gun off Joel to question me.

"I suppose curiosity got the better of me. I wanted to meet you, Ms. Ashwell." Joel waves the gun at Mitchell. "Him I don't care about, but it seems you two are attached at the hip."

"You're not getting out of here with Loralei," Mitchell says. "We know all about your plans."

"I suppose sticking around does make Elijah's death pointless." Joel laughs. "But it was fun. I can't deny that. The way the life drained out of him as I twisted that knife in his gut."

"You've wanted to do that for years," I say. "You don't think it was pointless at all. You've always wanted what Elijah had. You were jealous of him."

Joel's eyes narrow, and his jaw clenches. "I have what he couldn't get in the end. See for yourself." He raises the hand with the lantern to illuminate a figure lying on the ground about twenty feet away. I can't see her face, but it's definitely Loralei.

"What did you drug her with?" I ask.

Joel laughs. "Very good, Ms. Ashwell. Did you see me steal the pills they used to give me in the hospital? Or are you guessing? I admit I'm not clear on how your abilities work."

I'm not about to tell him things pop into my mind. I have a feeling the same happens to him, but his is in a psychotic maniac way and I don't want him comparing my abilities to his sick visions of a better life. "Why her? Is it just her connection to Elijah?"

"At first it was, but then I discovered she's a lot like me. She was pretending to be who everyone wanted her to be. I pretended for a long time."

"Until you got caught killing animals," Mitchell says. "We're well aware."

Joel laughs again, clearly amused and not at all worried about how this will end. Does he really think he can kill us both and get out of here alive?

"I feel like you're trying to keep me talking, Detective Brennan." Joel moves closer, his head cocked at an odd angle, making him look even crazier—if that's possible. "Let's talk about you for a second. You seem awfully confident despite my gun being trained on you. Why is that?"

"We're not alone, Joel. Even if you somehow manage to get past us, you won't do it with Loralei and you won't get out of this tunnel without being shot or put in handcuffs." Mitchell bobs a shoulder. "One way or another, you won't harm another person."

"What about you two? I think I'm at an advantage here. Unlike you, I don't have to wait to pull this trigger."

"What makes you think I have to?" Mitchell asks.

This comment brings a huge smile to Joel's face. "You're one of the good guys. You follow rules. You wouldn't shoot a man without being provoked."

"You're pointing a gun at my head. I've already been provoked."

"Now you're just proving my point about being a good guy even more. What's stopping you from putting a bullet in my head, Detective?" Joel takes another step, and Mitchell steadies his gun.

"One more step and I'll pull the trigger."

"Is that so? What if I aim the gun at her head?" Joel tips his head in my direction.

"He pulls the trigger before you can even point the gun at me," I say.

Joel continues to stare down Mitchell, but he addresses me. "Did you see that?"

He doesn't know I can't see the future. "Why don't you give it a try and find out," I say with as much conviction as I can muster.

"I'm quick on the trigger. I can shoot him and then you before you can blink."

"This is your last chance to drop your weapon before I shoot," Mitchell says.

"I'm not going to do that, and you're not going to shoot me either."

Something sends tingles down my spine. Joel lured us here because he has a backup plan. How didn't I see it sooner? "You don't intend to leave here alive," I say.

"Maybe you *are* good, Ms. Ashwell. After your last comment about your supposed vision of the future, I thought you might be a fraud."

"What are you talking about, Piper?" Mitchell asks me.

"If you shoot him, we'll all die."

"That's right," Joel says. "I have explosives strapped to my chest. Enough to cause another cave-in and kill us all. Now it would be tragic to lose everything after all the trouble I've gone through to be with Loralei, but it's an ending I'm willing to accept."

"What do you want?" Mitchell asks, going right into negotiation mode. "My phone won't work here, so I can't call off my backup and get you out of these tunnels without running into them."

"You can't. But she can." He juts his chin in my direction. "My original plan was to use Loralei as a human shield, but it seems I may have given her one too many pills. She hasn't woken up yet, and having to carry her out wouldn't suit my needs at the current time."

"You're not touching Piper," Mitchell says, but now that we all know he can't shoot Joel, the threat of the gun aimed at Joel holds no power.

"She is important to you, isn't she? And not just to you but to the entire police department. That's why my plan will work."

"There's only one way to know if it will work," I say, taking a step toward him.

"Piper, stop!" Mitchell yells.

Joel turns his gun on me, not the least bit threatened by Mitchell anymore. "What are you up to, Ms. Ashwell?"

"I can tell you if your plan will work, but I need to touch you to see it." The thought of coming in direct contact with this man makes my flesh crawl, but what other choice do I have? If I can touch him, I might be able to see something that could help or maybe I could even rip that bomb off him. But how would I keep the bomb from detonating? I know nothing about disarming explosives.

"Forgive me for being skeptical, but why would you need to touch me?" Joel asks.

"My strengths lie in reading energy when I touch objects and people. That's how I found you. I have your grandfather's pocket watch."

"Then why don't you use it now?" he asks, calling my bluff about needing to touch him specifically.

"It's not on me. I didn't want to touch it after I saw what you did to Elijah." I can say it with conviction since it's true, and he doesn't need to know Mitchell has the watch in his pocket.

Joel smiles. "I agree to your terms, Ms. Ashwell." He lowers the lantern to the ground and extends his hand to me.

"Piper, don't!" Mitchell yells, but we both know he can't stop me or Joel right now. The explosives on Joel's chest have rendered Mitchell powerless.

I reach for Joel's hand, and Joel begins to hum "The Music of the Night." Is this what I saw in my dream? Did I actually have a vision of the future? His fingers are cold to the touch as we first make contact. Then he yanks me toward him, wrapping one arm around my head and pressing the tip of the gun to my temple.

"I can't read you if I'm under duress," I say. "It blocks my abilities."

"I'm sure you can manage."

"If you hurt her..." Mitchell's threat hangs in the air between us.

"I'm waiting, Ms. Ashwell," Joel says.

I take a deep breath and place my right palm on his arm, which is under my neck. I lock eyes with Mitchell. The fear in his features couldn't be more apparent. I close my eyes and focus on allowing the vision to come to me. The

186

problem is I'm still not good at seeing the future. As much as I try to expand on that part of my abilities, I haven't been able to make it work for anything of any real significance.

I'm going to have to bluff my way through this. I take note of Joel's position. He has the explosive strapped to his chest, so he's holding me slightly to his side. I have no idea if him falling backward would detonate the bomb or if it requires a chest shot. I'm also not sure I could turn and catch him without hitting the bomb myself before he falls to the floor, so a shot to his head might not work either.

Think, Piper!

Loralei. She's the answer.

I open my eyes. "Loralei," I say.

Mitchell's eyes go to her form on the ground.

"Joel, she's going to wake up."

"How do I know you're not lying?" he asks.

"You wanted me to have a vision, and I did. I saw her wake up. I saw her plead with you to take her away from all of this. You were right about her. She's a lot like you. The reason why she never ended up with Elijah was because he wasn't enough for her. You are, though. You need Mitchell and I to get you both out of here. You can have everything you've worked for, but you need to listen to me."

"Piper, we can't let him leave," Mitchell says, and I'm not sure if he's playing along or if he thinks I really did manage to see the future. Either way, it's helping my plan.

"Joel, look. She just stirred," I lie since he's still focused on Mitchell.

"How do I know this isn't a trick?" Joel screams.

"Go to her. See for yourself," I say.

Joel doesn't release his grip on me as he steps backward toward Loralei's body. Mitchell follows us, his gun still on Joel. "This is getting tedious," Joel says, and my hand on his arm allows me to see what's inside his mind. He's going to shoot Mitchell. Joel presses the trigger at the same time as I yank him to his right.

The bullet lodges in the wall behind Mitchell, and Mitchell charges Joel.

"No!" I yell, breaking free from Joel and stopping Mitchell.

"Enough!" Joel volleys his gun between us.

I can only think of one thing to do. I grab the gun from Mitchell's hand and aim it at Loralei. "Drop your gun, or I'll shoot her," I say, hoping I'm even holding the gun correctly since I've never fired one in my life. My father always said I should learn how to shoot because of the line of work I'm in, but I could never bring myself to do it. Maybe he was right all along.

"You wouldn't shoot her," Joel says.

"You want to know what I really saw?" I ask him, moving closer to Loralei. "I saw her waking, asking you to take her away, and then me shooting her."

"No!" Joel screams and bangs his gun against his forehead. He's completely losing it.

"Let's talk this through," Mitchell says, trying to shield me with his body so Joel doesn't just shoot me on the spot.

A new idea comes to me. And finally, it's one that might actually work. I can't shoot this gun. If I do, Joel will kill us both. It was stupid of me. Mitchell needs the gun, but he can't try to kill Joel.

With Mitchell blocking me from Joel's view, I press the gun into his right hand. "Aim for his gun hand," I whisper. "Drop it, Joel, or I'll kill her. If we're going to die down here, I'll make sure you watch her die first," I yell, trying to keep Joel from knowing I no longer have the gun.

Mitchell plays along, keeping his right hand at his side

concealed from view. "She'll do it. She's a good shot, too. I've been to the shooting range with her." He holds up his empty left hand. "No one has to die. Let's all walk out of here together."

"You don't get to make the rules," Joel yells, raising his gun at Mitchell.

Everything happens so fast after that. Mitchell pushes me backward, sending me toppling to the ground. Two shots fire. I'm almost afraid to see what happened, but Joel's cries pierce the air and metal clinks against the concrete floor.

Mitchell's shot was accurate. Joel is cradling his gun hand, which is bleeding pretty badly. Mitchell rushes at him, but Joel presses his good hand, covered in blood now, to his chest.

"Don't move, or I'll detonate this!" Joel screams.

I scurry backward toward Loralei. Her chest is rising and falling. I shake her gently. "Loralei," I whisper while I continue to shake her. Her eyelids flutter open.

Mitchell and Joel are yelling at each other, completely oblivious to what I'm doing.

"Loralei, I need you to listen to me. We're in trouble, and if you want to get out of here alive, I need you to ask Joel to take you away from here."

Her expression is dazed. She has no idea what I'm talking about. Has he had her drugged the entire time?

"Please do as I ask. I need you to trust me."

She doesn't even know who I am. I flick my gaze in Joel's direction. She follows my gaze, and her eyes widen.

"If you don't do this, we'll all die in here. He's already killed Elijah."

That does it. At the mention of Elijah's name, Loralei sits up.

"Joel, look!" I yell, getting his attention.

"Loralei?" he asks.

She looks at me, and I give her the slightest, almost imperceptible, nod.

"Joel." Her voice is raspy from not having spoken. "Take me away from here," she says, repeating my exact words.

Joel eyes me suspiciously.

"You're hurt," Loralei says. "Let me see."

I couldn't have planned this better. Loralei's self-preservation instincts are great.

"It's okay, Joel," I say. "I lied earlier. You were right. I never could have shot her. I only said it in an act of desperation."

"Joel. Come here," Loralei says.

"Mitchell, stand down," I say.

Luckily, he listens. He lowers his gun to his side and let's Joel pass.

"Loralei, you're awake. I was afraid I'd given you too many sedatives."

"I'm okay. Tired, though."

"She'll need to be carried out of here," I say. "I guess Mitchell will have to do it since you can't."

"No one touches her," Joel says.

"I can't walk," Loralei plays along. Why she's trusting me when she doesn't know anything about me, I'm not sure. I'm extremely grateful for it, though.

Joel bends down to her and takes her hand, raising it to his lips.

I pat my chest, trying to convey to Loralei that he's rigged with explosives.

She doesn't understand, though, and she reaches for his chest. He pulls away. "No. You can't touch me there."

"She's scared, Joel. She wants you to hold her," I say.

"I can't. We won't get out of here if I remove the explosives."

Loralei backs away, suddenly terrified.

"You're scaring her. Take them off."

Loralei nods. "Take them off," she repeats.

Joel's face hardens. "This is a trick!" He stands up abruptly, but Mitchell is ready with his handcuffs. Joel thrashes. At this rate, he'll detonate the bomb despite his hands being cuffed behind him.

I rip open the buttons on the front of his shirt, exposing the bomb. Loralei screams behind me.

I touch the wire closest to me and concentrate harder than I've ever concentrated before. In my mind, I see Joel assembling the bomb. Step by step. Without opening my eyes, I repeat the actions in reverse order while Mitchell holds Joel still. As soon as I'm finished, I open my eyes.

It's over.

CHAPTER TWENTY-ONE

The light of day never looked so beautiful when Mitchell finds the switch to open the drawer in the mausoleum and let us out. The place is filled with police. Even Harry is here, barking at Joel.

Two officers take Joel into custody, reading him his rights. Another attends to Loralei, who thankfully can walk, but she's a complete mess after the ordeal. She nearly lost it when we had to step over Elijah's body.

The entire way out of the tunnel, Joel tried to plead with her, tell her how much he loved her. She wouldn't hear it. She called him every synonym for insane she could think of, which included two that hadn't even crossed my mind.

"We had no idea where you went," Officer Wallace says. "We had to bring Harry in. He picked up on your scent, but we couldn't figure out how to get to you in there."

"We only found the entrance thanks to Piper," Mitchell says. "She's the best detective we've got, even if she isn't officially on the force."

"Thank you, Ms. Ashwell." Officer Wallace nods to me.

"Elijah Graham is dead inside the tunnel. Someone will

need to go get his body." I don't ever plan to go back in there again.

"We'll take it from here," Officer Andrews says.

Mitchell and I walk out of the mausoleum, and I'm not surprised when I see Dad sitting in his car on the long driveway that curves all through the cemetery. I walk right over to him, and he lowers the window.

"I see I missed all the fun," he says.

He wouldn't have been able to handle what happened down there. Not when Joel had his gun pressed to my temple. If it were anyone else, Dad would have been the picture of calm and done what he had to. But I'm his little girl. He probably would have shot Joel and sent the entire place up in an explosion of body parts.

"Never a dull moment with Piper," Mitchell says. "She did great. As usual."

"I think I'm going to take some vacation days after that case," I say.

"You earned a vacation." Mitchell puts his hand on my shoulder, earning him a look from Dad, and he quickly removes it.

"Well, boys, I'm going home to take a nice long bath and wash off the craziness of this case."

"That could take a while," Mitchell says. "I'd better get you home."

———

I take a full week off before returning to the office. Jezebel is happy about it. She doesn't seem to mind that I'm her new owner. I guess she's been through a lot with Elijah and Mindy's divorce and then being left alone when Elijah went after Joel. She seems to like the quiet, pampered life she has with me.

"Time for Mommy to go back to work, Jez," I tell her, holding her face in my hands.

She gives me those big, brown sad eyes she's perfected.

"Don't look at me like that. I'll be home at lunchtime to take you for a walk, okay?" I kiss the top of her head.

She licks my chin twice before I can pull away.

Dad and Mitchell are both at the office when I arrive. I toss my purse on my desk. "Don't even tell me we have another case to collaborate on," I say. "Where's my coffee?"

Mitchell reaches for the carrier on Dad's desk. "Marcia says hello. She's missed you over the past few weeks."

"You're a liar. I saw her four times when I bought new books." I take a sip of the large toasted almond.

"I'm not lying. She mentioned she saw you those times, but she's been worried about you. I guess she thought you were shielding her from how you're really doing."

"I'll make sure she knows I'm fine. So, tell me what's brought you back here so soon," I say to Mitchell as I slump down in my chair.

"I figured you'd want to know what happened after we arrested Joel."

I nod.

"He requested to see his former doctor."

"He's pleading insanity?" I ask, unable to believe he might get away with murdering multiple people and kidnapping Loralei.

"He did. He was sent back to the psychiatric hospital, but he never made it through his first night there. He threatened one of the nurses. Scared her practically to death. She caved and gave him the bottle of medication he requested."

"He committed suicide," I say, knowing it's true.

Mitchell nods. "They found him the next morning. The nurse quit, but she's being held under investigation for her part in his death."

"What about Loralei?" I ask. "Is she okay?"

"She filed for an annulment," Dad says.

I figured she'd do that. Even with Elijah out of the picture, she couldn't see herself with Steven.

"Steven wasn't all that surprised," Mitchell says. "Loralei is moving away. She said she can't live up to the person her family wants her to be, so she needs to be free of them, too."

"I guess it's case closed then. All the lose ends are tied up," I say.

"There is one more thing," Mitchell says. "Loralei's friend Catherine came to us. She confessed that she tried to stop Loralei from marrying Steven. Catherine felt Loralei and Elijah were meant to be."

"What was the point of her confessing that?" I ask.

"Guilt I suppose. She felt like if she hadn't interfered, Loralei might have gone on her honeymoon as planned instead of insisting on meeting Steven at the airport." Dad adjusts his burgundy tie. "Guilt makes people confess strange things. She feels like she drove Loralei away, too."

"I think from now on, I'm only associating with dogs. They're so much easier to read and understand," I say.

"How is Jezebel?" Mitchell asks, sitting forward in his seat.

"Living large the way every dog should."

"We should set up a play date with Max," Dad says. "Bring her to Ashwell family dinner night tomorrow."

"I think she'd love that."

Mitchell rubs his hands together. "All right. Home-cooked meal at the Ashwell household."

Dad and I exchange a glance before looking at him.

"What?" Mitchell asks.

"We're never getting rid of you, are we?" Dad asks.

"He's like a fungus," I say. "He won't go away, but he kind of grows on you."

Mitchell smiles.

I extend one finger at him as I hold my coffee cup midair. "I said *kind of*. Don't let it go to your head."

He leans back in the seat. "Whatever you say, boss."

"That's more like it," I say. "Now, tell me about the case that really brought you here."

"You didn't even have to read me to know that," Mitchell says.

"I'm starting to figure you out."

He smirks. "This case is quite the doozy."

Aren't they all?

———

If you enjoyed the book, please consider leaving a review.

And look for *Drastic Crimes Call for Drastic Insights*, coming soon! https://www.kellyhashway.com/piper-ashwell-psychic-p-i

You can stay up-to-date on all of Kelly Hashway's new releases by signing up for her newsletter: https://bit.ly/2ISdgCU

Reignited

After Loving You (New Adult romance)

Campus Crush (New Adult romance)

Perfect For You (Young Adult contemporary romance)

Falling For You (Free prequel novella to *Perfect For You*)

Our Little Secret (Young Adult contemporary romance)

ACKNOWLEDGMENTS

I have to thank Patricia Bradley first for always having great suggestions and edits, but also for sending me notes saying I'm becoming her favorite mystery author. Thank you for loving my books as much as I do while still pushing me to make them better.

To my family and friends, your support never goes unnoticed or unappreciated. Thank you for allowing me to share my books with you. To Kelly's Cozy Corner, you guys are amazing for taking this journey with me and helping me spread the word about my books.

And to my readers, I couldn't do this without you.

ABOUT THE AUTHOR

Kelly Hashway fully admits to being one of the most accident-prone people on the planet, but that didn't stop her from jumping out of an airplane at ten thousand feet one Halloween. Maybe it was growing up reading R.L. Stine's Fear Street books that instilled a love of all things scary and a desire to live in a world filled with supernatural creatures, but she spends her days writing speculative fiction and is a *USA Today* bestselling author. Kelly is also *USA Today* bestselling romance author Ashelyn Drake. When she's not writing, Kelly works as an editor and also as Mom, which she believes is a job title that deserves to be capitalized.

facebook.com/KellyHashwayCozyMysteryAuthor

twitter.com/kellyhashway

instagram.com/khashway

bookbub.com/authors/kelly-hashway

Printed in Great Britain
by Amazon

42329450R00123